"In the tradition of Truman Capote's *Other Voices, Other Rooms*, Ben Nitaokpulo taps the now-neglected vein of the slow Southern narrative. Floating in time, *Northaw* could be set in any period."
- Marissa Marcus

"A revealing narrative of poverty, ignorance, exploitation, discrimination, neglect and the failure of successive governments to bring education, welfare and care to the oppressed."
- Malcolm X. Mawdsley

"A testament to the human spirit, freedom, and the spirit of America reminiscent of *To Kill a Mocking Bird* and *Catcher in the Rye*."
- Jordan Rucker

Copyright © Michael Reidy 2024

Cover photograph by Colin Ellis
Design by Bespoke Designs,
Yelverton, Devonshire.

ISBN: 9798333330901

Northaw

a novel by

Ben Nitaokpulo

Compiled and Edited
by Cordelia Madison
and Michael Reidy

PARKMAN HOUSE
BOSTON
2024

Publisher's Note

Ben Nitaokpulo's book reached us by a circuitous route, propelled by a single-minded lady, Cordelia "Dolly" Madison.

Miss Madison showed up at the Philadelphia offices of Lattimer & Co. struggling under the weight of a large, beaten-up corrugated carton. When she persuaded our American Fiction director, Missy Sharpe, to open it, she found more than a hundred small 48-page notebooks with tan covers along with loose sheets and several spiral bound notebooks.

The only reason Miss Sharpe gave these a second look was because Miss Madison believed it to be the unknown first novel by the late Ben Nitaokpulo.

Nitaokpulo was one of the very few early 21st century bloggers to become a serious, commercially published novelist. Several of his books have won awards, and while having many admirers – among the critics and the public – he never achieved best-seller status, and never was offered a television or film deal.

He had begun as a travel blogger, visiting small towns across the United States and several in Canada. While of mixed race, dominantly Choctaw Indian, he considered himself an American first and that was one of the qualities that won him readers.

Nitaokpulo gives much of his own story in *Northaw*, so it need not be repeated here.

Miss Madison was a close friend of Nitaokpulo at the time of the events of the book. A fellow blogger and media freelancer, she maintained contact with him as he continued his travels.

When he left Demopolis, Alabama, for the last time, he stored some of his things with his sister who lived with her husband and children in their old family home.

Several years after his death (presumed from a snakebite, near the ironically named Mayday, Colorado, while exploring Dead Wood Gulch) his sister contacted Miss Madison to see if she wanted – or at least wanted to look through – the things that had been left with her.

It took Misses Madison and Sharpe six months to read everything, decide which sections were related to *Northaw*, and try to rebuild the book.

It was a job reminiscent of the task faced by Edward Aswell after the death of Thomas Wolfe. The parallel is apt because it was the act of going home again that led to the writing of *Northaw*.

August 2024
Paris

To Lahoma, always

The past is never dead. It's not even past.

William Faulkner
Requiem for a Nun

x

Preface

I don't think many bloggers write novels, and this is my first attempt. We'll see how it goes. Up to now, the longest piece I've written is about two thousand words. I've written some newspaper and magazine articles, but mostly I write blogs about traveling in America.

I grew up with Jack Kerouac, Bill Bryson and Garrison Keillor's memories of the United States. I later discovered William LeastHeat-Moon's wonderful *Blue Highways,* and that cemented my decision to go on an endless road trip to places I couldn't imagine in the United States.

It was pretty successful, too. I learned to play the social media, was invited to speak on local radio and once or twice on television. Later, a publisher approached me to put a collection of blogs together and published them as *Who'd Want to Live Here?* It generated a lot of interest and got me on more local talk shows talking about stuff I didn't know much about.

America's big enough to let people write about it pretty much all the time. I knew I wasn't going to be as good as Kerouac, Bryson, Keillor or Moon, but that didn't matter. I was seeing a different America, not the one of their generations. And that's another reason not to lose faith.

The diversity of the land and climate is matched by the diversity of its people. Even now, in a time when things are nearly as polarized as they were in the run up to the Civil War, there rests a belief and faith in the vision of the United States. It seems to have gone underground in some places, but the heartland has earned its name, and I share the optimism of those ordinary people who believe that those values will reassert themselves.

The most important thing my travels did was to lead me home to Demopolis, Alabama, to rest, take stock and prepare for whatever came next. It was also where, just about the time I was getting restless again, I met Lahoma.

BN
Demopolis

1

Ben tells me this is my story, and I should tell it as I like. My name is Lahoma. Lahoma Atoka Lefever. It sounds interesting, but the truth is, I'm no one from nowheres. I haven't been anywhere, and it's nice to dream but the truth is, I never wanted to go anywhere. Not that I'm particularly happy here, but I know myself well enough to know that I probably wouldn't be more happy anywhere else.

So where is here?

I live near Demopolis. Demopolis itself ain't no great place. Once it had a theatre, busy markets, steamers landing and loading almost every day, and all sorts of things. It was busiest during the war when there were supply depots and things for our soldiers, and roads and steamboats to take them North to fight, or South to better hospitals.

Demopolis was a junction with the boats on the Tombigbee and Black Warrior. They go all the way to Columbus and Tuscaloosa. Maybe farther. Later, there were trains, but I never rode one.

"Lahoma" means "the people" in Choctaw. "Atoka" means "ball ground," which I really don't understand. "Lefever" is French. That's how I like to think of myself, though people say I don't look French.

People are confusing. At least to me, and I've seen a lot of them.

The story is that in the old times, a bunch of people who had supported Boneypart had to hide from the people who took over from him. They left France, came to America and took a boat up the Tombigbee to a place near Demopolis. People tell me they called it the Vine and Olive Colony, but I don't believe them.

"How could they call it that?" I asked them. "Vine and olive ain't French."

Even I know that.

Well, the land wasn't much good for vines *or* olives, but they got permission to keep the land anyway. This was way back in the eighteen-twennies or thereabouts. From what I've been told there was a lot of land. But, as I said, it wasn't good for vines or olives. It kept flooding, people kept squatting on it, but this was the Black Belt and worth stayin', although a lot of them gave up and went down to Mobile, or Norleans. Some say that a bunch of them went back to France.

But one of the ones who stayed was called Lefever and his family built Northaw. That's where I live – at least some of the time. Of course, back then when half of them went home, Northaw was only half built. Brick walls, unfinished pillars, like stumps, and piles of wood and lots of people working. Many were slaves, but they was from all over and everyone, even Monsieur Lefever an his family, lived in small wood cabins. Madame Lefever didn't like it much.

Northaw

When the big house was ready, they tore down the cabins and used the wood for floors, cupboards, shelves, tables, doors and stairs. Some boards were even hauled up to make the roof.

Funny to think that what was once a floor become a roof.

Monsieur Lefever, he called the farm a plantation when he was in town, but they told me it weren't nothing like what could be seen from the river steamers: fields as far as you could see, pink with plum blossom, blue with beans, yellow with corn, or white with cotton.

Northaw plantation grew all those things, too, – and tobacco – but because the way the Black Warrior and Tombigbee wandered everywhere, the fields were small and could flood. It made the earth rich, but not the Lefevers.

Northaw ain't much these days, but it's a lot more than it was in my first memories. I remember hearing a lot of talks about how things should be done. There wasn't many arguments as most of the men had never built anything this big before.

People was talking all sorts of languages, too. Monsieur Lefever was speaking French, Creole and some English. I knew French and Creole best back then.

There was someone who did all the measuring and counting, and one of the slaves named Jonah – who had built a brick plantation in Mobile or Norleans, somewheres

5

far away. He knew how to mix cement for the bricks and set them strong.

As the house grew, Jonah, the brickman, also worked the ropes and pulleys to haul the timber to the top floors. He called the ropes "lines" which Mam said was because he'd work on ships. I thought slaves only worked in the fields and on steamboats, an' only helped build things when they needed to. I never knew one before him as worked on ships at sea.

The pillars grew every day. There were six showin' on each side 'cept the back. When the pillars was ten feet tall, the counting man said they were as straight as he'd ever seen. People didn't mind working with Jonah and doing what he told them.

Jonah lived in a cabin two along from where Mam and I were. After supper, if the weather was good, the men would sit around outside and smoke and talk. Sometimes they would drink, too, but Monsieur Lefever didn't like that 'cept on Saturday night.

Sometimes the women would sit behind them, sew, or smoke and have their own conversations. Some of the young boys would try to get close to the circle, but the men didn't want them there, so they'd go down to the river and smoke an' some girls would go with them. Most girls would stay near the women and sometimes learn to sew, but my friend Jody and I would crawl under the cabins and get as close to the men as possible and listen to their stories.

Sometimes Monsieur Lefever would join them. He had good stories about France and his uncle, crossing the ocean, and, once, being in battles. Sometimes, he'd talk about the house, but only if someone asked him.

I liked Jonah's stories best. While Monsieur Lefever talked about travel and adventure, it was all too far away for me to think about. Jonah's stories were about the Black Warrior River, the Tombigbee, and sometimes the Alabama an' even the Mississippi.

Jonah told stories about Norleans and the people, noise, colors, the gamblers, sleeping on rooftops when it was hot and loading the boats again. One night, he told a story that I never forgot.

"The men had been playing cards and drinkin' half the night in the saloon," he said. "It was so late that even the piano player had gone home, but four or five men were still in the game. We was sittin' outside with the horses so as to take the boss home. He was in there, standing by the table, smokin' a cigar and watchin' the game."

Jonah's voice was so deep and smooth, it was hard to believe it came from someone so thin – he was strong an' all – but pretty long with no fat I ever saw. He ate well. This is what people have forgot. Even though he was a slave, smart owners kept the important ones fed to get good work from them. He always had good meals, not like Jody and me who couldn't be depended on to do much work at our ages.

"Eventually, Mr. Skitters and Mr. Carterer had everyone's money and were the last two playin'."

I knew those names, Mr. Skitters had a plantation south of Demopolis, an' I had heard about Mr. Carterer from Monsieur Lefever. Apparently he had business in Mobile – what sort I didn't know till later – and Monsieur didn't like him much.

"All of a sudden, voices were raised, there was sounds of furniture falling over and you could hear coins hittin' the floor and rollin' all over.

"The two men came out accusing each other of cheatin'," Jonah continued, and you could hear all the mosquitos in the silence as we waited for him to go on.

"When they stumbled on to the porch and down into the street, I 'spected to see fists raised an' some swings taken. But, their voices went very quiet once they were in the middle of the street. Everyone from the saloon came out – no one had dared to touch the money on the floor – an' before the last one was on the porch, Mr. Skitters and Mr. Carterer was twenty paces away from each other and raising their pistols."

"Didn't anyone try to stop them?" one of the older boys asked.

Jonah turned towards the boy slowly – it was Buck Market – and fixed him with a stare that held him as a snake's would.

"Jus' how do you think you'd stop a man with a raised pistol?"

A few men gave nervous laughs. Buck shrunk back and looked like he wanted to disappear, but he wanted to hear the end of the story more, so he hid his embarrassment and leaned forward to listen again.

"In the dark, it was hard to see who fired first," Jonah said. "It was too dark to see any smoke and the flashes and the explosions were too close together to tell."

He paused and seemed to listen to the crickets and frogs. A log shifted in the fire and startled those sitting near it.

"Both men stood still for a moment, and I thought they'd both missed, but then Mr. Skitters, straight as a board, fell forward. Several men ran towards him, but two men went to Mr. Carterer and arrested him for murder.

"They hanged him two weeks later."

No one said a word for several minutes, then Jonah stood up and walked to his cabin, saying nothing. I was surprised I slept at all that night. The scene is real in my head and keeps comin' back, so I half believe that I was right there on the porch with Jonah.

Sometimes evil creeps up and wraps itself around you like a snake.

I had heard the men and older boys talking of going over to Demopolis to meet the steamboats.

They were built with a broad lip that made the deck come right onto the land while the boat was still in very shallow water. They'd buy what was needed for the house and load it onto a flatboat. They had to be careful so the flatboat that men pushed with poles didn't get too low and let water onto the deck and spoil the goods. When they got back to Northaw, everyone would help unload. Jody and I would roll small barrels of nails, being too small to do much else than get in the way. Later we'd carry sugar, flour, and big bags of vegetables that we didn't grow.

The building of the house went on for several seasons. It seemed like half my life. It took a long time because the crops and the animals needed tending. There was fishing, too. When I was old enough, they put me in charge of the goats.

I was braver by then and would get closer to the men when they was telling stories. I'd keep very still so people didn't notice me.

There was a lot of gossip that didn't interest me because I already knew who was sweet on who, and who was seeing someone they shouldn't.

One of the men was telling stories about traveling to Mobile and staying in a hotel with soft pillows, warm blankets and a mattress that he just sank into "like pudding," he said. I hadn't seen a mattress then. I slept on straw – or hay if there was enough – covered with a burlap sack or old blanket. The hay was softer and smelt better.

Northaw

I remember when the house was near finished. It looked big and tall and wide. It had taken so long to build that I was about twelve, maybe thirteen, and building it was just about all I could remember. The pillars held the balconies that went all around the upper floor and held the roof. I couldn't see it, of course, but they told me that it sat on the house with a peak in the middle. There were chimneys here and there to keep the winter chill off, but the brick walls and all the shade from the roof and balcony made it cool in the summer.

From what I saw of the big rooms inside, they had lots of windows, high ceilings and pretty fireplaces. Some were iron and some were wood with some carvings from Selma.

What I do remember is that there was not a lot of furniture. That would come, Monsieur said, he had to wait until the harvest came in and he could sell some crops.

By now, the cabins we'd been living in were sagging and drafty. Many of the cabins had been taken apart to build the big house, so new buildings for the slaves and other workers had to be built.

Mam said we'd be moving into the big house soon, as we was family. I didn't understand how or why, but I liked the idea.

Northaw

Ben's Notes

After several years of wandering around America – mostly in the Northwest and Southwest – and writing my pieces, returning to Demopolis was odd to say the least. Like all places, it had changed but was the same. Writing about places you know is much harder than writing about places you're seeing for the first time. Those places have no memories or associations with people or experiences, and the residents of new places are less apt to make a fuss and take umbrage at what a "foreigner" writes.

For me, Demopolis was still home and as I wandered about its streets I remembered where my friends lived, where we played, where their fathers worked, where I went to school, played sports, shopped, kissed my first girlfriend, and all those things.

I actually came back to Demopolis for a rest, not to write, and it's never a good idea to write about your hometown. I never found the place particularly interesting, though like everywhere else, it had a history.

It grew from the colony that Lahoma mentioned, and its place as a stop on the river and later its railroads gave it its tenuous permanence. Even today, most of the railroad crossings are at street level and have the same simple crossed board signs that they had 170 years ago.

The sense I had on my visit was that Demopolis had no reason left to be there. The river boats were gone, what trains there were didn't stop. Even the Rooster Bridge – one of the towns only claims to fame – was gone.

The population peaked about five years ago, and though it is four-and-a-half times larger than after the war for the Southern Republic, it is well below the rate of inflation.

More worryingly for the town, is the rate that the population is decreasing and so are the reasons for staying. The shipping is gone, the plantations are gone, and with it the cotton warehouses and loading docks for the steamboats and railroads. Gone are the cotton ginners, cleaners, seed processors and the few mills for carding and spinning. The supporting people are gone, too, along with the cotton brokers, shipping companies and freight forwarders and all who worked for them.

Northaw

There's little entertainment. The theaters and movie houses have closed, many of the diners and restaurants are shut; the hotels are gone, and the furniture factory has closed.

There is an airport now, but it's pretty quiet with only a dozen or so "operations" per day. Two of those movements could be moving a single engine Piper into the hangar for repairs and then back to the field. There is some good news. The vast cement works to the east of town continues to operate while large private and public construction and wood and paper product industries operate near the airport.

Looking at the town, it didn't seem that it was the first choice of residence for these employees. My impression was anecdotally confirmed when I had lunch one day at one of the few remaining places to eat in Demopolis itself.

TripAdvisor says there are nineteen places to eat in Demopolis, but fourteen of them are on Route 80 which is a by-pass, or the fastest way out of town, depending on your inclination. Two more are on the other through route, Highway 43.

Located opposite the Public Square, an unprepossessing storefront reveals an interior reminiscent of a New England diner.

I sat at the counter and ordered a late breakfast with eggs, sausage patties, biscuits and gravy. After some friendly chit-chat when I mentioned to Angel that I was born here, she gave me a small dish of grits.

"How long are you stayin'?" she asked.

"Not long."

"No one ever does," she said, refilling my coffee.

"Apart from the cement factory and the plants around the airport, what do people here do?"

"Same as you: leave."

With the aging population, middle-aged people stuck around to look after parents, aunts and uncles, and commuted to work in Selma, Meridian, Linden and other places.

My own father had been a master craftsman in the now-closed furniture factory, and my mother worked part-time in a local bakery once my sister and I were in junior high.

We weren't rich, but were comfortable enough with an old two story brick house near the center that my father had renovated until it was one of the best smaller properties in town. My sister and her family still live in it.

Northaw

The various publishers of my articles over the years have made much of my Choctaw heritage. I am certainly not ashamed of it, but it has been exaggerated to the point that various websites would have you believe I'm a full-blooded Native American.

One day, I'll set the record fully straight but in this part of the world, full-blooded anything is a rarity. Both my mother and father's side were mixed race many generations back, but I'd bet there were full-blooded Frenchmen in the line more recently than full-blooded Choctaw – or Alabama, Cherokee, or Chickasaw.

It would take an anthropologist to identify any non-Caucasian features in me, but I do appear to have a mild suntan in the middle of winter, though these days, people assume it's fake. My sister doesn't even show that and has to buy her tan, though we both have straight, Indian-black hair.

Somewhere back there, there may have been a Negro ancestor, too. Legitimate or not, who knows, and I don't really care.

I've always thought of myself as an American. A native (small 'N') American because a) I was born here, and b) because my family were all born here, back to about the time of the War of 1812 and, obviously, before.

My pedigree (or lack of it) had nothing to do with my travels around the United States or spending my time writing about it.

So, where does this passion for travel come from?

I think it was something my ninth grade geography teacher said. It was a spontaneous comment made in reply to the not unusual question, "Why do we have to study geography?"

Mr. Rush was a brilliant, deep man. I never saw him angry or flustered. Looking back, he was a man comfortable in his own skin. The big question was why he spent his life (which proved to be very long) in Marengo County?

His answer to the flippant question spoke volumes of the man:

"Geography is about places. Places you know and places you may never see. Take Demopolis – "

"I wish someone would!" someone shouted.

Mr. Rush just smiled and continued.

"Why is it here?" he asked. "It might have been somewhere someone pitched a tent for a night or two and then moved on – but someone stayed and a town grew. Why?"

For a few moments, he'd captured the imagination of all thirty-two of us. Another student filled the rhetorical silence and called out:

"The river."

Mr. Rush nodded.

"And what else?"

"The earth is good."

And the lesson resumed, but it ignited in me a passion for place and what a particular place means to particular people.

The result was that I studied geography at the University of Alabama in Tuscaloosa, not having the slightest idea what I'd do with it.

You will have noticed that asking questions like, "Why here?" and, "Who would come to this particular place?" leads very quickly to history and philosophy.

Northaw

2 One of the nice things about Demopolis is that they left a wide strip of land along the river that belongs to the town. That way, everyone can share the river.

I like sittin' on the bank near where the steamboats used to load and unload. There were a lot of them, and there were carts and long wagons stacked high with bales either going to or coming from the warehouses. There would also be sacks of cotton seeds, barrels of cotton oil and cotton cakes.

Loading the boats it would look like you couldn't fit another bale anywhere but sometimes I'd count thirty more being loaded.

One day while I was watchin' the river and day-dreaming, I saw a young man not far from me, standing on the bank, about twenty feet back from the river, and just watchin' it like I was. As I looked at him, it was as if I knew what he was thinkin', and I wondered if he knew what I was thinkin'. Probably not, as I don't think he'd yet noticed me.

He stood there a long time. People today often stop and just look for a while before moving on to do things they think is important. They'll pause and glance and think that's looking. I wonder if they ever notice anything.

Even though the river runs close to Northaw, you can never see it because it's up a creek aways and trees block the view. But here, the river is broad and straight.

When the steamboats were running you could see the smoke as it came round the bend about four miles up river. Of course, this was in winter on clear days with blue skies. Otherwise, it was too hazy and skies were dirty white. The whole bulge of land in Sumter County down to the ferry landing was cultivated and treeless. Now, its all forests, and you can't see, but there ain't no steamboats, neither.

Some days you can smell the river even when you can't see it. The smells are different depending on the time of year. In the winter, sometimes it just smells cold. In the spring, you can smell the manure that's washed off the fields, other times in late summer, you get the smell of the green slime, dead fish and rotting plants on the bottom. It ain't nice, but that's the smell that comes up the inlets around Northaw, so there's no escapin' it. It gets into your head and you just keep on smellin' it even though the river might have stopped smellin' days ago.

There were times when the river got pizened and the dead fish smelled for weeks, but once that flushed out, it were good.

I was tellin' about meeting Ben.

I watched him standing on the bank, thinkin'. Well, he may not have been thinkin' but jus' lookin'. I do that sometimes, for hours. Doesn't matter what I'm lookin' at

– a tree stump, a rock in the river, one of the old fireplaces, or the collapsed pieces of an old wagon. I just get lost in them. Sometimes it feels like for a very long time.

There's something about the way he's standing. He looks sort of defeated. He's standing, but he's remembering things he'd rather forget. I seen plenty of that.

I'm not scared of much anymore – 'cept loud noises and people shouting – so I make my way slowly towards him. I'm sure he sees me, so I try not to look too crazy. When I get close enough I ask:

"Have you ever traveled on the river?"

He turns to me and for a moment looks at me, workin' out what I want, but I'm used to that. I don't make any excuses and take a good look at him, too.

He looks tired, he's almost as skinny as I am, and his eyes are kind. That surprises me a little as people who look that tired usually have a hard look. Maybe he had a good time getting tired.

"Only once, when I was about ten or eleven. An old steamboat ran a leisure trip one summer," he said. "We boarded up at the boat launching area. The steamboat came within a few feet of the shore and we walked up some wide planks that were just leaning against the boat."

"That's the way they used to do it," I said. " There used to be a ferry landing right there. It connected to a road on the other side that ran along the river. Sumter Road."

He looked at me and I could see him wondering how I knew this.

"Tell me more about your trip. Did you go up or down the river?"

"It was a good trip," he said, remembering. "We went up to Twelve Mile Bend and sailed right around it. Forkland, past the Ravine. We tried to see Lamberth's Mound, but there were too many trees."

"Rattlesnake Bend," I said.

"We had lunch on board. The saloon looked great and there was even some music for a while."

He sounded excited, but I felt a chill. It was the mention of the music in the saloon, I think. I don't know why, but I was shaking. He didn't notice but was still staring up the river.

"As a ten-year-old, I thought the steamboat was wonderful with the black smoke pouring out and the steady power of the wheel," he said. "I did get a bit scared at one point. We'd moved into the shadow of the trees and someone pointed to some rocks and said, 'that's Haunted Point.'

"The person he was with asked why it was called that and he said, 'Believe me, you don't want to know.'"

He looked at me with a big smile.

"Now, I know that no one is really sure why it's called that," he said, laughing. "There are lots of stories – all different."

Northaw

There's only one real one, I thought. An' you're not ready to hear it.

"Did you like being on the river?" I asked.

"Out on deck, especially on the top gallery away from the noise apart from the splashing of the wheel, it was serenely quiet."

We stood quietly for a few minutes.

"Do you believe in haunted places?" I asked.

He looked at me, and I wondered what he really saw. He made no comment but turned back to the river.

"I believe people may be haunted," he said.

I didn't know how to reply.

I'd have to think about that.

I wanted to get back to Northaw. I don't like being away from it for long. No matter what I see in and around Demopolis and other places, Northaw draws me home.

Northaw

Ben's Notes

I hadn't thought about that boat trip in years. It was a good memory. Thinking about it, it must have been a Fourth of July celebration because the steamer was decorated in red white and blue bunting, and my father was with us.

At that point, Lahoma hadn't even told me her name. She'd stirred up old memories, good ones, mostly, and I need time to think about them. It was rude, but I was so lost in my own thoughts I didn't hear her say anything more or even notice that she'd left.

In my first year at the University of Alabama, I spent a long time studying maps and charts of the river around Demopolis. This was not because I was fascinated by the town, but because my father had suggested it might be a good way to hone my skills as a geographer. I'd be able to check out features I identified first hand and develop my eye for reading maps.

He was right, and looking at the details of the area was rewarding. One of the things that struck me was that nearly all of the dozens of streams, inlets and large areas of water were simply labeled Tombigbee River or Black Warrior River, when in reality, they were distinct and often distant features.

I was even able to answer questions about why the land to the east of town along the Black Warrior River hadn't been developed to handle trade from Tuscaloosa.

The transport of cotton was the reason for Demopolis' existence. It might have been a more pleasant place had it been founded on olives and vines as originally intended.

Between Columbus, Mississippi and Mobile, there were more than three hundred landings where steamboats could pull up along the shore. Some were municipal landings and others were on private plantations or warehouses.

At Demopolis and other places along the river, there used to be bluffs some up to eighty feet tall. Curiously, that is where the Indian landings were and the early French settlers landed at their foot, too. Ecor Blanc – or white cliffs – was the common name.

After building the dam and locks, the cliffs were reduced by fifty feet. It flooded the fringes of Demopolis, submerging the Confederate cemetery and obliterating the Sumter ferry landing near the present-day yacht basin.

People have always been vague about whether the soldiers' bodies were relocated, but I suspect not. Just more ghosts for the Tombigbee.

Going back to the high bluffs on the river, there were often cotton chutes. Slaves would roll the bales – about 400 pounds each – down the slide where stevedores on the steamboats would stack them for the voyage south. On the larger boats, more than three thousand bales would be piled up.

While this seems a curious practice, it made more sense than running a wagon train to the boats and manhandled down the bluffs or, where the river met the shore, manhandled up an often narrow gangplank, though that was done, too.

The dangerous handling and loading was done by immigrant workers – often Irish – because they were less valuable than slaves.

There were also vast warehouses where smaller loads would be aggregated with the farmers sharing the cost of the loading.

Today, whatever the faults of the town or its future, the old decision to leave a wide strip of land along the river for public use was wise.

It was a commercial decision, of course, to enable the largest possible number of steamboats to stop and load at any one time. It would also increase the chances that the boats would stop at the town and not just slide by to a more welcoming landing.

Many boats did pass by because they were already full, laden from towns and plantations on the upper rivers.

☙

It's time to stop this travelog and history lesson, but these were the stories I grew up with. Coming back to see these places brought them to mind, and they have formed a useful procrastination to delay writing about the girl.

She was an odd one, and to find her standing next to me gave me a start and a bit of a chill. There was nothing threatening about her, but I'd been so lost in my thoughts that I was unaware of her until she was next to me.

My first impressions were that she was small, looked very young and somehow old-fashioned. I guessed her to be about twenty, but it wouldn't surprise me to learn she was only fifteen. I judged her to be about five feet tall, but she wore her hair up and secured with a large pin. There was a lot of it, and it was black and parted in the middle with loops covering her ears before being braided and pinned at her crown. The dark hair, her complexion and features indicated to me that there was more than Indian blood in her.

Her voice was small, too, though she spoke clearly and with a strong Alabama accent. A local girl. She hadn't said much, but it might be interesting to see her again and hear her story. No doubt she could tell me more about Demopolis.

Northaw

3 It's not like me to talk to strangers, but he looked thoughtful, and it was in a very public place. I still worry about things like that. Normally, I'd never speak to anyone until I was spoken to. That didn't do, not for people like me. But now, there's not anyone around to talk to me, so it really doesn't matter.

After leaving Ben – although I didn't yet know his name – I returned to Northaw. I didn't leave there much anymore; don't know why I did this time. I think I just felt restless.

In the old days, up to the War Between the States, it took an hour or so to row or paddle to the inlet that led to Northaw. Going down river was always faster, of course, and if the river was flooded, it could take a lot longer to get back. If you were in a small boat, you'd paddle until you were tired, then pull into the shore and hang onto a branch until you caught your breath, then went another few hundred yards before pullin' in again. Mostly, I went on the flatboats, poled by slaves.

Monsieur Lefever bought a flatboat from a man who had shipped cotton from Aberdeen and sold it to Mr. Webb. Mr. Webb stored the cotton then shipped it on a steamboat to Mobile.

The man sold the flatboat because there was no way to get it back upstream to Aberdeen or anywheres else. People took flatboats all they way down to Mobile, sold the cotton and then sold the boat for the timber and rode home on a steamboat. If the flatboat hadn't been damaged by rocks, deadheads or by crashin' into other boats, you could get most of your money back. Even if it had been damaged, someone could buy a few year's firewood.

Anyways, Monsieur Lefever saw Mr. Webb's and had the idea that he can use it to float his cotton from Northaw to Demopolis then push it back to Northaw with poles. It seemed to work and it took fewer men to push than a keel boat and carried a lot more cotton.

Northaw is just a mile or so up the Black Warrior River towards Tuscaloosa, so the flatboat could be landed on the north bank of Demopolis. Eventually, Mr. Webb built a landing and warehouse there to serve boats from Tuscaloosa and plantations along the way.

There being a lot of water around Northaw when the river flooded, all the children learned how to paddle boats – like pirogues and dumpy row boats – and how to fish. Sometimes, we'd gather wild berries. The berries were mostly used at Northaw, but we'd catch enough fish so that some could be taken to town and sold. The price wasn't much because everyone was near the river, but not everyone wanted to spend their time fishin'. Besides, it kept us out of trouble and Monsieur Lefever said it earned enough to feed us.

Jody was great at catchin' fish. Ticklin' fish was a favorite trick. I wasn't good at it and caught most with a

Northaw

net or pole. If people were tryin' to tickle, I'd get sent away because I'd giggle and move like I was the one bein' tickled.

The fish would be pickled, smoked, dried, or salted. Mostly, they'd be fried or grilled fresh on the fires. I never knew how they decided to do what with them.

The younger children began their fishin' by learnin' to catch water dogs to use as live bait for bigger fish like wide mouth bass or crappies. We'd use small nets on poles to catch the water dogs and put them in a pail or jars with water. Some of the older boys would put them on the ground and try to race them, since they had legs, but they'd be told off as a tired or dead water dog wouldn't catch nothin'.

While the slaves were polling the flatboat, the other men would fish off the side. They'd fish when the flatboat docked while the slaves unloaded the cotton.

I once asked Badger how he felt about the men fishing while he had to work, pushing the boat and unloading a ton of cotton. He said there were no hard feeling' as the men gave half the catch to those doin' the work.

That was one thing that was true. As long as Monsieur was alive, near as I could tell, no one at Northaw was ever afraid. If they was, I never heard nothing about it, and Jody didn't neither.

One day, we heard Monsieur talkin' to some business men at Northaw. They were surprised to see the slaves jus' getting' on with their work and with no one drivin' them.

35

Sure, someone would check every so often, but they had work to do, too. I'd seen drivin' in town and on other plantations – run by nice folk – and it were horrible.

Monsieur answered the men, best as I can remember, "You see any houses near here? You see any plantations nearby? That's because we're alone. In the winter, we're on a big island.

"I don't want to be murdered in my bed and they don't want to be beaten, threatened or made to work when no one in his right mind would want to. I try to be fair, an' they try not to murder me."

The slaves weren't the same as him and Madame Lefever, but they were warmer – or cooler – dryer and better fed than others on nearby plantations and farms. That didn't mean that they weren't beaten sometimes, but only after Monsieur listened to their stories and made his mind up about what happened. He didn't beat them himself. That was done by whoever had caught the slave doin' what he shouldn't or not doin' what he should. Sometimes, it were another slave did the beatin'.

I didn't like it, so I didn't watch, but lots did. Jody and Buck would tell stories about it for days and tease me because I didn't like it.

Later, I learned that the reason Monsieur had different people do the beating was so they all knew how terrible it were. It also made the others respect him for doing what needed to be done.

Northaw

Beatings was pretty rare, compared to other places. I learned what that really meant when I was older. Some people thought Monsieur was soft. They'd point to me when I'd come into Demopolis to help with the buying and say Monsieur was bad for taking his bastards around with him and for not being meaner.

Buck put it best.

"Monsieur thinks it's bad if a slave gets hold of alcohol and gets drunk, but he won't beat him unless he hurts someone or breaks something."

Of course, there was the case of Mr. Buxton. He was one of the managers; replaced Mr. Tilson when he retired. Mr. Tilson was well-liked because he'd take time to show the slaves how to do things, and when he was keeping them moving in the fields, he'd actually sing with them. Not many whites did that.

Anyways, Mr. Buxton was mean. I don't know why, but he'd push and pinch people, shout and threaten. According to Buck Market, a lot of the other white hands didn't like him either. Buck Market said the men said, "He was too free with the wrong women."

I wasn't sure what that meant, but he said it again six months later after Mr. Buxton had his accident with the cotton gin. After that, he went down to Mobile to get his arm fixed and never came back.

Mam and I were somehow different. We weren't treated like slaves, but we weren't free, neither. I didn't understand why until I was about twelve. Jody told me first, then a few months later, Mam did. She thought it was time I had a better idea what to expect from life.

I wasn't really sure what it all meant. I could still come and go as I had done – though Mam wanted me to be to able to read, write and do numbers. I could see how that could be useful, having watched Jonah and the numbers man. They'd do measuring and figuring and write numbers on boards with charcoal or on the ground with sticks.

To me, those numbers were like magic spells: they'd write them an' set to work and a doorway would appear, or some windows, and staircases that went from the ground to the next level perfectly.

It seem' to me that to have that power would be special.

Ben's Notes

Lahoma told me her story in bits, and piecing things together was becoming difficult. She seemed to have no sense of time, and her talk about the past was a complicated fantasy. She didn't seem to be dangerous, but I kept hoping she'd give some facts that I could check.

It was after Lahoma and I talked several times – always at the same place near where the land sloped gently to the river – that my sister invited me to dinner.

I got along well with Leah (her full name was Panoliyah which just means "cotton" in Choctaw). There are lots of different ways of spelling it – most of them simpler – but my parents liked elaborate names. I'm not going to tell you what Ben is short for.

She and her husband, Bob, have two children, Bella and Stevie. They're both busy but I've been seeing them for various meals at their home or somewhere near. Stevie and Bella like tacos, so Route 80 is a feast for them.

On Friday, I was at my regular diner enjoying pancakes and coffee and Leah came in and asked me for dinner that night.

"You're not one for formalities," I said. "Is this an occasion?"

Leah laughed easily. As a sister growing up, she was always good humored. Even as a teenager, she was never too fussy, moody, or difficult. She wasn't a goody-goody, either, and the two of us got into our share of trouble – together and individually.

"I'm just having a few friends over and thought you might like a good meal," she said. "Come at six."

Eating dinner at six used to be late in Demopolis. Only the rich and pretentious ate at six-thirty, or even seven. The decline of local industry and business means that more people commute further, so supper is usually later now than it was when we were growing up.

While Leah and Bob had no fancy ideas, they liked to do things properly. Meals were at the table with no television and now, no cell phones, and generally well-behaved children. Leah wasn't an ambitious cook, but I knew I'd be well fed.

Since my arrival back in Demopolis, Leah and I had been in contact daily with calls and text messages and met several times a week for coffee, lunch, or I'd go to the school and meet her to collect the children.

Considering the difference in ages and the time we'd been apart, we were pretty close, though I know she doesn't like what I do much and wishes I'd get "a real job."

Almost as soon as I arrived at the house, I knew Leah had some plan.

After greeting Bob and looking a Bella's new drawing and Stevie's latest Lego construction, I noticed that the table was set for six. Hardly enough space for "a few friends."

"Leah!" I called, as I went it to the kitchen, to challenge her.

"I'm glad you could come," she said, knowing well that I had nothing else to do.

"I thought you were having a group of people."

She handed me an iced tea. It wasn't iced tea weather, but it's what they drank all the time.

"Change of plans," she said, turning back to making a salad.

"Who's coming?"

"Don't fuss, Ben," she said. "Go sit down with Bob and relax."

"*Leah*, you're not trying to fix me up with one of your friends again, are you?"

She turned to me with an impatient look.

"I only did that twice and it was in high school," she almost scolded. "A big sister needs to look after her little brother sometimes. Besides, I think you'll get on just fine with Dolly."

Dolly.

My heart sank.

"Forget it! I'm thirty and don't need your help."

"Well, I can't go on letting you sit by the river on your own for hours," she said. "People will start to think you're not right in the head."

"Goodbye," I said, and turned to leave.

The sound of the doorbell stopped me.

"That will be Dolly now," Leah said brightly, totally ignoring what I just said.

Bob answered the door, and a happy voice greeted Bob, spoke to the children and then advanced towards Leah and me as we went to meet her.

"This is Cordelia Madison," she said. "Everyone calls her Dolly. And this is my little brother, Ben."

I already suspected the personality was big, but Dolly herself was imposing. She was about five-nine, and though she wasn't heavy, what there was was solid. I thought that most of her presence was posture, but later she told me she'd been captain of her school lacrosse team.

She was pretty, too, in a modest way. She wore no makeup that I could see, and her dark hair was parted down the middle, emphasizing the subtle Indian features of her face. High cheek bones, strong nose, wide-set eyes – all the stereotypes, but true.

"Hi, Ben," she said. She had very little Alabama accent but had the friendliness. "I think I've seen you around. Been back long?"

"A coupla weeks."

"Dolly does blogs and things, too," Leah said, and left us to get a drink for her.

The small talk continued over dinner – a meatloaf from one of my mother's recipes – and continued until Bella and Stevie had enough and disappeared upstairs.

"Do you know many people in town anymore?" Dolly asked me.

Dolly had a voice that suited her size, but it was big in richness, not in volume. Her words were well-articulated, not the casual, sloppy speech of most people – including myself – but a speech with more inflection than usually heard in America – even in Alabama.

"I tried looking up a few. Most have left. Two old friends are at the cement works and another still does some business up and down the river."

Dolly smiled with some special knowledge.

"I asked because I've seen you sitting by the river with a girl. More than once."

Leah looked up quickly.

"Ben? You never said anything," she said. "Whenever I've seen you by the river, you were alone."

"There's nothing to say," I said. "I walk around, read, write, watch the river, and have coffee and some meals in the diner, or drive down to Route 80."

"And the girl?" Leah pushed.

"She's just a strange lonely girl who talks to me sometimes," I said, feebly. "She seems to know a lot about Demopolis in the old days."

It was now Dolly's turn to look up.

"I'm very interested in local history," she said, seriously. "I blog about it and would like to write a book about Demopolis sometime."

"It'll be pretty thin," Bob said.

Dolly laughed with the rest of us.

"Every town has a surprisingly rich history," I said.

Dolly nodded and for the rest of the meal, we talked about various places we'd been and written about, and my sister looked pleased.

Northaw

4 I was not too bad with numbers. Writing and readin' were a problem for me. It's a good thing that Ben does the writin' an' then reads it back to me, and I tell him what he got wrong.

Back when I was learnin', there were four of us an' we were taught for a bit each day by Jonah, though he was busy workin' and couldn't spend more than twenty minutes with us. The rest of the numbers time was taught by Peony.

Peony was another slave, and she was old, and big, and would sit in her chair. She ran the kitchen in Northaw but often stayed in that chair, tellin' everyone else how t' mix, measure, knead dough, cook meat, bake fish an' everything else. She usually had a bowl of somethin' in her lap and would shell peas, peel potatoes, carrots, apples, peaches an' anything else that needed peelin'.

It wasn't until later that I learned she had come to Northaw after Mr. Skeeters was killed and his plantation, Bower Mount, was sold and broken up with the land and slaves going to the neighboring plantations and homesteads.

It was hard to tell how old Peony was, but she was probably 'bout the same age as Monsieur. He had dined at Bower Mount many times and said it was the best food he'd had in Alabama. He felt sorry that she'd be sold with the rest of Mr. Skeeter's things and probably to someone who would never discover how well she could cook. She'd be cheap because she was old and wouldn't likely be sold 'cept as part of a job lot. He thought Northaw could do with a good cook, and that it would please Madame.

Monsieur clearly liked Peony, and I had the feelin' that he knew her, maybe even before she went to Bower Mount. I asked Mam, but she told me to mind my business.

Even though she spent much of her time in the chair giving orders, she certainly wasn't lazy. She made things using almost every bit of food, and it was good so there was no waste. When Peony did get out of her chair, she could move surprisingly fast – which she did if people came into the kitchen to steal fruit or sweet biscuits.

She came when the ground floor of Northaw was just getting the floor above it put on and Monsieur Lefever, Jonah, and the countin' man would meet with Peony an' she told 'em what she wanted in her kitchen an' where she wanted it.

Madame would appear during these meetings and make a fuss about her husband taking advice from slaves. Jody and I would peek through the unglazed windows and listen to her rantin' for ten minutes without a breath.

"Why doesn't he tell her to shut up?" Jody whispered to me.

Jody acted a bit older than me but didn't seem to have the same common sense. Still, Jody was my closest friend.

"It wouldn't be polite," I explained. "Monsieur has his faults, but he's mostly fair and polite."

Jody started laughing, so we had to leave the window and run into the trees.

"An' Monsieur has always been polite to you, has he?" Jody said, with a grand gesture.

"Hush!" I said. "Monsieur treats us all right. You've seen some of the others with scars on their backs. He almost never does that. Jonah says that Monsieur isn't afraid of using everyone's special talent. That it doesn't matter whether they're a white or a slave. That's why he listens to Jonah and Peony was well as the countin' man and the others. It's another of his French ways."

Jody thought about this for a moment and looked very concentrated, the asked,

"An' what do you think of being a slave?"

I looked into Jody's face with surprise.

"Hush. Not now!"

"But you must think about it?"

"'Course I thought about it, but not all the time," I said, angry because it were somethin' I didn't like thinkin' about.

"We was talking about the noise Madame was making," I said, tryin' to get back to the matter. "I don't supposed she's cooked an edible meal in her whole life."

We giggled.

"Well, I 'spect Peony will get her way and spend the rest of her life by the kitchen fire bossing people."

49

While Northaw was being built, there were two makeshift kitchens among all the huts we all lived in. Monsieur lived in his own hut, and Madame and their son lived in Mobile until the house was finished. They came up to see how the house was progressing, and, according to Jonah, it was an opportunity for her to tell Monsieur how he'd done it all wrong.

"She's a lady with strong ideas," Jonah said one evening, after Monsieur had gone into Demopolis to put her back on a steamboat. "He lets her go on, then carries on what he's been doin'."

Of course, there were no white men around when he said this. Even so, if they wanted that house finished, they needed Jonah.

Anyways, it was Peony who took over the numbers when Jonah's time was up. Jonah taught us more about how to measure board, calc'late the area of a field, how to measure the speed of the river, and how to work out how many bricks it would take to make a wall.

When things got more advanced we learned about how many four hundred pound bales of cotton could be loaded onto Monsieur's flatboat and how many trips it would have to make to move a hundred bales to Demopolis for loading onto the Mobile steamboat. To make it hard, we had to figure how long the loading and unloading was, and when the trips would have to start to get all the cotton to the steamboat landing.

I could do this but Badger and Buck Market were really good at it. As for Jody – well, Jody could do it, but wasn't interested.

One day, Jody was daydreaming, Jonah asked about plans for the future, and Jody just shrugged. I never seen Jonah get mad before. He was talkin' about belts and whippins, and bein' starved.

Now, I loved Jody, but tis was no way to behave. When the lesson was over, Jody got a piece of my mind, too.

Jody wasn't any more interested in what Peony taught us which was about weights and measures for food. How it was different for wet and dry things like flour, meal and seed, and oil, milk, water, juice and so on. We learned about bushels, pecks, barrels, pints, quarts, gallons, and how whiskey was made and measured. Useful things.

Ben laughed hard when I told him about the still behind the huts. Jody couldn't wait to steal some, but I'd smelled the breaths of men who'd been drinkin', so didn't want anything to do with it.

Peony was also full of stories about root magic: spells, haints, ghosts, and how to put a bit of graveyard dirt into the bottles on the bottle trees.

But that's enough for now.

Northaw

Ben's Notes

I learned enough about Dolly at my sister's to arrange to meet her for coffee a few days later. While I was not traveling, I continued to write and make plans for future travels. I spent time in the library, too, and it reminded me of my high school days, though it's been renovated several times since then.

It's in the Ulmer furniture store building next to the Marengo Theater, which I also knew well in my youth. The main room has a number of large tables which are ideal for spreading out books and papers, and writing. I've been using the maps, but since meeting Lahoma, I've been looking into the genealogy section and trying to make some sense of her story. It's obviously a family story that's been handed down and garbled along the way, but there might just be the odd bit of truth that I can pin down.

I usually do everything myself, but there are some things I think Dolly might know, and she said she saw me talking to Lahoma.

My trouble is that I talk to so few people that when I do, I can't stop talking. What I really want to do is pick Dolly's brain about the local history she said she knew.

I was about to leave the library to meet her, when a name leapt off the page of the book I'd been looking at – Henri Jacques Lefebvre.

There was just one mention and that was in a list of some of the original settlers of the Vine and Olive Colony.

That gave me a single thread that I could follow.

☙

I met Dolly at the diner for a late coffee which I hoped might turn into lunch. In spite of pushing us together, my sister soon monopolized the conversation with Dolly the other night, and I talked about baseball and the state of Demopolis with Bob. He was hardworking, easy going and seemed to get on with my sister which made everything fine in my book.

What I did learn was that Dolly had a local history blog and was doing what Rufus Ward was writing about in Columbus and the upper Tombigbee region. She kept her work focused on Demopolis and the immediate area and wrote in a more "contemporary style." She'd met Ward several times and considered him a mentor and the ultimate source for Alabama information that didn't make the history books.

I had come across his articles before and found more during my work in the library.

One thing I liked immediately about Dolly was that she always looked cheerful. At my sister's, I'd put it down to their friendship and regular contact with the family, but she greeted me the same way when she entered the diner and sat in the booth with me.

"I really enjoyed Friday," she said, after sitting down. "I like your sister, and think the children are fun – and interesting."

We chatted about the evening over coffee, then ordered lunch.

"You said you grew up in Demopolis," I began. You're about my age, so how is it that I don't know you and my sister does?"

Dolly laughed.

"I didn't go to school in Demopolis. I was at Baylor," she said. "Then I was at 'The Capstone'."

"Let me guess: psychology?"

"Oh, it could have easily been, but my father made me see sense and major in history," she said, with a coy smile.

55

"Do you regret it?"

"Not at all – it's made my career so far."

"The blog. What's it called," I asked.

"'Alabama Dreamin'."

I smiled.

"Ah, The Mamas and the Papas. What's it about?"

"Anything I want," she said, not quite smugly. "I focus on Black Belt history and things around Demopolis."

I nodded.

"Are you part Indian?"

"Creek."

"You know Leah and I are part Choctaw – who knows how much."

Dolly nodded.

"We met by accident at the farmers' market, started talking about the price and quality of tomatoes. It took about three minutes before we shared our heritage," she said. "To be honest, she almost feels like a sister. I know, different tribes – but it's hard to be sure without DNA testing, and who really wants to know?"

"Tell me more of what you do," I said, after our food was served.

"I hope I hide it, but I'm pretty spoiled. As far as my parents are concerned, I should be doing ladylike things until I get married," she said.

"And that's imminent?"

"Fortunately, no," she said, with a laugh. "That's why I'm doing the blog and other social media, the writing for papers and tourist magazines, and the rare TV bits. I'm hoping that one of them will take off so I can be independent. How do you manage it?"

We were eating club sandwiches and fries (Dolly substituted fries for a salad, but still stole several of mine).

I laughed.

"Do we know each other well enough to share such secrets?" I asked.

She laughed, too.

"I won't tell if you don't," she said.

"I get temporary work for a month or so. I've done all sorts of things, building work, short-order cooking, cashier work, warehouse work. There's quite a bit of very short-term work which few people want. I don't need a lot of money, just enough to pay for gas and a cheap room."

"And the blog?"

"It pays for two really good meals each month – or a week of spaghetti."

Dolly put her fork down and looked at me.

"I really admire – and envy – you," she said. "I told you, I was spoiled. I still live with my parents. They have a house in The Cove that backs onto the Whitfield Canal."

"Very swish."

Dolly looked embarrassed but resigned.

"The biggest problem – apart from being marriage fodder – is that my father has political ambitions, so I *always* have to be on my best behavior."

"And you find that difficult?" I teased.

She suddenly looked serious.

"You said the other night that you were interested in the old plantations that were around here."

I nodded.

"I might be able to help you."

"I've been looking for the old maps with the properties marked, but I haven't found much."

"There weren't that many immediately around here," she said. "You'll know the main ones: Foscue House, Gaineswood, Bluff Hall. Did you think there were more? I sense you're looking for something in particular."

Northaw

5 I was never afraid of much. First of all, because there weren't nothin' much to be afraid of at Northaw, and secondly because Monsieur Lefever wouldn't let anything bad happen to me – or to most of us livin' on the plantation.

Mam, Buck, Jody and even Peony would protect me, too. 'Bout the worst things that happened at Northaw was someone gettin' snake bit. Once an alligator took one of the dogs. 'Part from that, not much bad seemed to happen. There might be fights if some of the men got to drinkin', sometimes strangers would come trying to swindle Monsieur, but he was too smart for that.

One man I heard called Mr. Wilson came trying to buy or sell land. Northaw was almost finished, and they were livin' in it, so that must have been around 1845 – I know you like dates, Ben. I was about seven or eight. Of course, I didn't know the story until I was much older, and then only heard it in pieces.

Monsieur had met Wilson in Mobile when he was down on business, and they'd got on fine. Wilson said he'd be making his way up the Tombigbee and maybe head to Columbus, or Tuscaloosa doin' business along the way.

They met up at the Demopolis Hotel, where Wilson was stayin', an' Monsieur invited him for dinner. The boat was near Webb's warehouse and the ferry and ford, and it was less than two miles to Northaw from the hotel. I never heard what boat they took. It might have been the rowing boat, but it could have been the pole boat.

Peony says that even though it was just the four of them – Madame and Monsieur, one of the managers, and Wilson – that it was an especially fine dinner with some of the French wine that Monsieur had.

There was much laughter an' noise, and a small group gathered on the ground below the balcony, as they often did. Peony would bring out some leftovers from upstairs and we'd have more to eat from it. No one ever told Monsieur that she did this. He probably wouldn't mind, but Madame would have a fit.

Havin' one of the managers for dinner weren't unusual. Sometimes they'd talk to some of the leadin' men about what needed to be done the next day or ask them to keep someone in line.

Peony had brought out some fruit and cake left from dinner an' said that Madame had gone to her room and the men were drinkin' whiskey and talkin' business. We were gathered under the balcony, an' those not eatin' fruit took to smokin' their pipes. So, we all moved to the corner of the building so their smoke wouldn't blow up into the house where Madame would smell it, or Monsieur would come out on the balcony and tell us to go to our quarters.

We was listenin' to someone telling us about a new steamboat due to come up the river that was bigger than any we'd seen. It was longer and broader and more

Northaw

powerful than any boat that had come up the river before. It was supposed to be able to carry a thousand bales of cotton and lots of people in luxury.

This set 'em to arguing about if it could carry that much cotton. Surely, the story got exaggerated on its way upriver. A thousand bales was 'bout two hundred tons, they said. No steamboat could carry that; that were more than the steamboat weighted, besides, the river was too shallow.

They were discussing how it might be done, depending on how wide the boat was. By this time, I'd done enough numbers with Peony and Buck to know what they were talkin' about.

Our talkin' must have been low, as we heard Monsieur shouting upstairs. We fell silent and listened. No one ever agreed what Monsieur was shouting, but he sure wasn't happy with Mr. Wilson.

We then heard another voice that must have been Wilson's, then there was a scream from Madame Lefever, who must have come back. (We all knew her screaming.) Then Wilson backed onto the balcony and a gunshot startled us and Mr. Wilson jumped backwards, hit the railing, lost his balance and fell to the ground, about five feet from the nearest men with us.

We heard Madame screaming some more, then Monsieur shouted at her and she was quiet.

The men on the ground gathered round the body, but it was Peony who rushed out and put her head on Wilson's chest and listened for a heartbeat. She stood up – which wasn't easy for her from the ground – and shook her head.

By this time, Monsieur was down with us.

"Roll him over," he instructed the manager.

"When he did, we all saw another pistol lying under the body."

"Is it cocked?" Monsieur asked.

The manager picked it up carefully and held it to the light from the house.

"Yes, sir."

"Good. Get rid of him," he said.

Four of the men carried him off. I later heard from Jody that they had put him in the rowboat until morning, then rowed him to one of the islands and buried him. I also heard that the next time Monsieur Lefever went to Demopolis, he reported the shooting and said that there were many witnesses who had seen the cocked pistol when the body was moved. Some said that Monsieur handed it in, others that he kept it.

It became one of them things that no one talks about, but everyone knows every detail.

Peony and others said that Wilson's evil had got into the house because the porch ceilings hadn't been painted blue. Wilson's evil might still be around, and none of us wanted that. Monsieur and Madame didn't believe in haints and at first refused to paint the ceilings, but when some of the oldest slaves, including Peony, talked to him, he saw the advantage of doing something if only to keep everyone calm.

He asked questions about how high the spirits could go, and eventually agreed to paint the ceiling that overhanged the ground floor. Since that's where I lived, I was happy. If those upstairs wanted to risk it, well, that was white folk's business.

In a week or two, men set to paintin' a blue wash on the ceiling. It's something of a magic potion itself with lime, indigo and water and oils that had catnip, basil and rosemary soaking in it for a week before mixing. Peony mixed the herbs, and the men mixed the lime and indigo.

She said that even if there were no evil spirits, it would help keep the insects away.

Later, when I walked around the edge of the garden around the house, just over the walls and fences, I saw dead tree branches stuck in the ground with blue bottles on them.

They hadn't been there before Mr. Wilson was kilt.

Ben's Notes

Dolly's open nature led me to believe that she was being honest with me. She certainly seemed to know about Demopolis and the area. My quandary was deciding whether and what to tell her about Lahoma.

On the positive side, it would be more fun to investigate this with someone who also had a strong interest in history and the area. Against that were all sorts of risks ranging from being considered a fool for pursuing things that might just be fantasies spun by Lahoma, and trying to untangle the way she told me her story and trying to get it to make sense, to becoming involved in something that could restrict or curtail my travels.

Dolly's next question forced a decision.

She put her knife and fork down and stared at me seriously.

"Before we go any further, tell me about this girl I've seen you with a few times," she said. "I know me meeting you was your sister's idea, but I don't want to get involved in anything that's going to cause trouble."

She gave a smile and continued.

"I might not always please my father, but I don't break up relationships."

The fact that she said this without a hint of embarrassment told me a lot about Dolly.

I put my fork down and tried to look back at her in the way she'd looked at me.

"There is nothing between Lahoma and me," I sad. "She comes to talk to me, and I write down what she tells me."

Dolly, unexpectedly, laughed.

"Is that what a date with you is like, Ben?"

I realized how dumb that sounded and smiled.

"No, not really," I said. "So far, it's just her."

The waitress took our plates away, and Dolly asked for coffee.

I took a deep breath.

"Look. This could take a long time to explain," I began, "and I could do with someone to talk to about this – and her – and maybe do some research and field work."

"I'm ahead on my blog articles and have nothing else for a while," Dolly said. "I'm all yours."

I nodded.

Northaw

"Don't volunteer too quickly," I said. "I don't think this is dangerous, but it could get seriously strange."

I told her how I'd been sitting by the old landing and Lahoma had come up, sat next to me and asked about the river. I told her that she had said she was Lahoma Lefever and that I had just found a reference to Henri Jacques Lefebvre who had been part of the Vine and Olive Colony.

"So, the plantation you are looking for was his."

She said it as a statement, not a question.

"Do you know where it was?"

"Only that to get to it, you needed a boat," I said.

I told her about rowboats, flatboats and keel boats, most of which she knew.

"What does she look like?"

I shrugged my shoulders.

"She's young, about twenty, but could be a few years either way. She's part Choctaw, like her mother, and there maybe some Negro in there, too."

"Her mother? Is she still alive?" Dolly asked eagerly.

"Let's get out of here," I said. "This is where it gets strange."

We paid the bill and walked into the Public Square and found a bench.

"When Lahoma leaves me, it's hard to remember what she looks like," I said.

"And we females make such an effort!" Dolly joked, then saw how serious I was.

"I see her face – it's not that different from anyone else's around here with Indian blood," I said. "She has the straight black hair, fairly long – "

"Is it braided? Pinned? Cut in a fringe?"

"Sometimes it's just straight and parted down the middle and sometimes it's in an elaborate old-fashioned style. I mean antebellum old," I said. "I think it's very long. Mid-back. No makeup."

"Does she look healthy?"

"I suppose so. Hard to tell."

"What's she wearing?"

"I don't know. Sweatshirt, denim skirt – I've no idea."

Dolly shook her head, clearly annoyed with me.

"I hope I never need you as a defense witness," she said, in an exasperated tone. "Have you ever touched her? Has she touched you?"

"No."

"Didn't shake hands, brush a fly or leaf from her hair or clothes?"

"No."

"Does she wear *shoes*?"

"I never noticed. I suppose she does."

Dolly thought for a moment.

"Does she always come when you sit by the old landing?"

"Yes."

"Have you seen her anywhere else?"

I had to think, but then said no.

"If I sat by the landing with you, do you think she'd come?"

I shrugged again.

"Can we try it, or are you afraid it would frighten her away?"

I said nothing, not having what my mother would have called "the vaguest idea."

"Somehow, I think she would come if we were together," Dolly said.

"You think?"

She faced me again.

"Last Friday, your sister mentioned seeing you sitting alone on the bank, but when I've seen you there, you've always been with Lahoma.

"I think she needs to tell you her story, and my being there isn't going to stop her."

Northaw

6 One of the reasons I like Ben is that he doesn't ask many questions. He lets me talk. He's read me the pages that he's written for me, and I've asked him to fix some things, which he does. I hope he can put the story in order, so they make sense to someone. That's the trouble with memories, they won't stay put.

I was talkin' about the bottle trees that was more the Negro slaves' rootworkin' than the Indians, but Northaw was a mix-up, so all kinds of things happened together, and no one seemed to mind. Mam told me that the Choctaw people themselves was a mix up of tribes that came together, and the Creeks were the same.

That's the way she said it, "It's like little streams and creeks comin' together and comin' together until there's a river like the Black Warrior and then that comes together, too, with the Tombigbee.

I seen Ben with a girl. Another part-Indian. They don't know each other well but seem to get on all right. It's a shame because neither of them is finished their journeys. Ben's come back for a rest and she's about to set out for the first time. She's already decided but doesn't know it.

Ben keeps tryin' to put what I say in time order, but things don't work like that. Ideas group together naturally – at least in my head – and time just breaks them apart. Ben tried to tell me about cause and effect, and I can understand that up to a point, but ideas and feelings don't always do things in order. Not for me anyways.

Nothing ever came of shooting Mr. Wilson, and I never knew if he was buried or fed to the alligators. Once he was carried off, no one seemed to talk about it. Even Jody told me to just forget about it.

When I was about fifteen, the house was finished and furnished. Peony said Madame wanted to show off, and as the crop had done good, and the river stayed high enough to keep the steamboats comin', Monsieur gave in, and they had a great party.

That must have been at the end of summer as it was only slightly cooler, and the water was low. Mam told me of all the work to make things ready and perfect, and that included food and getting uniforms for all the servants. I'd heard that other plantations had them, but when it was jus' Madame, Monsieur and Pierre François, no one fussed.

Pierre François – who was only called that by Madame, he was still Petey to the rest of us and his father – was about a year older than I was. He thought he was important and could be a nuisance to everyone, but Peony and Jonah weren't afraid of keepin' him in order. Mam told me much later that Monsieur had given a number of the responsible slaves permission to keep him under control. As he grew older, he learned a lot from Jonah, and I never heard Petey say a bad word about him.

Northaw

Anyways, we all worked for days to get things ready for the big party. Monsieur was very well known as one related to the town's founders, and he was known on plantations and in counties up and down the river.

Extra rafts went to Demopolis for food and drink, for extra chairs and decorations. Madame had a dress made. She had wanted to make a trip to Norleans to get it. Monsieur said she could, but it would be a pity because she wouldn't get back until ten days after the party was over.

While men serving and helping people off the boats looked handsome in uniforms, the maids and girls my age wore dark green dresses. I liked mine but Mam thought it showed too much of my chest and tried to make it sit higher which only made it more uncomfortable.

Still, everything looked grand. Flowers, chairs on the lawn. Wine being brought out from the kitchen to people standing in the grounds.

Jody, for some reason had nothing to do with it and stayed out of sight the whole time.

My main job was supposed to be in the dining room, but I helped pass drinks around, escorted ladies to the privy, and tried to look busy. The other slaves would ask me to fetch things, so by the time we got to the dining room, I'd run three miles.

It was good to overhear people's comments about Northaw. It made a good impression, but the women didn't like it that you couldn't just walk into town but had to take a boat.

Madame looked really pretty, but someone said she'd look better in Paris than in Demopolis. I only told Jody that as it wouldn't be good for Madame to hear it.

Petey looked silly. Anyone could see that his mother had dressed him, not his father. He had a shirt with ruffs that Peony said would have looked good fifty years ago. He had buckled shoes, and a jacket that could have been a cadet's uniform. I'd seen some in Demopolis.

He just looked uncomfortable and told me so later.

The meal went well. The food was always good in the house, an' Peony had done her best. I knew there'd be plenty left over and some slaves would eat well later. At the end of the meal, some of the men stayed around the table, but others followed Monsieur on a tour of the house and gardens.

I was making a trip around the lawn picking up glasses that had been left behind when Petey jumped from behind the big old black gum tree by the edge of the lawn.

"Master Petey, what are you doin'?" I exclaimed, and he gave a big laugh.

"I'm moving about," he said. "Haven't been able to do that for hours."

"You did look uncomfortable at the table, Master Petey," I said.

He was lookin' at me funny. I thought.

"Petey Lefever, have you been drinkin'?" I demanded.

His face looked like he was tryin' to puzzle out if I was bein' out of place, or if I was jus' someone he'd played with growin' up talkin' like I always did.

"Might have been," he said.

I started back to the house, holding two empty glasses by their stems by my side.

"Lahoma!" he called, running after me.

I stopped, as was my duty.

"You're looking pretty tonight."

I knew that look.

"Thank you, Master Petey," I said, "but I have to get these glasses back. An' I strode off to the house.

He didn't follow all at once, and I had reached the door to the kitchen under the balcony an' was about to go in. The door was open because of the heat in the kitchen.

Petey ran up to me, pulled my arm an' said:

"I told you you were lookin' pretty," and gave me a big kiss.

Now, I'd been kissed before, but not by him, so I stood there looking like a wooden-top. At that moment, Peony came out. She must have heard us or was lookin' for me with the glasses to wash.

"Pierre François Lefever!" she shouted. "Leave your sister alone!"

Northaw

Ben's Notes

I accepted Dolly's suggestion that she sit with me near the bank to see if Lahoma would join us. I could see Dolly's argument: Lahoma had shown no signs of possessiveness or innuendo; her complete lack of physical contact demonstrated that. So, I was won over to the belief that Lahoma's urge to tell her story would override the presence of Dolly.

One problem was that Dolly wanted to read what I'd written about Lahoma before sitting on the bank with me. I didn't want to let her do that.

She was a blogger and a rising media type, and while I liked her – a lot – I wasn't ready to give her access to my notes and what I had written about Lahoma. I wanted this to me my book.

I rightly guessed that Dolly's interest in Lahoma and her story would keep her in the project – and with me – even if I denied her access to what I'd written.

Not that there was much.

I didn't want to tell Dolly, but rather than write a local color piece with a good helping of history, I was looking at a way of developing this yarn into a novel.

My first.

I was taking down Lahoma's narrative and trying to put it into an order that made sense but had not yet developed anything resembling a plot.

The research I had been able to do was rewarding, though I had not yet found much more than Henri Jacques Lefebre's name. It was my guess that Henri was the nephew of General Charles Lefebvre, Count Desnouettes. Had he been a son, there was a better chance that there would be a mention of him. There was a good chance that he was a Creole – in the original sense.

It was on this question and on the location of the as yet doubtful Northaw that Dolly could prove helpful.

I had enough now to ask Lahoma questions, but I didn't know how she'd respond, if at all. I'd have to be careful and use my questions as prompts, not as an interrogation. For all I knew, if questioned, she might vanish in a puff of steam.

At the moment, being with Dolly was exciting. Neither of us knew where this was going to go, but we were both interested in the stories of the area, and I was eager to pin them to things that Lahoma talked about in her imaginative world.

I began by asking Dolly about things I'd already researched a little. Rafts, keel boats, steamboats and the nature of the river.

She demonstrated far greater knowledge than I had.

"We see the river as we always have," she said. "It's there, and we think it always has been, but earlier – in the 1800s, and especially before the war between the states – it was a lot different."

I had to concentrate because I found myself thinking of her voice again instead of what she was saying. She sensed this and turned to me.

"Go on," I said, trying not to look a fool.

"I was saying that we don't really *look* at the river in the way they did in the past. To them, it was rather like the way we think about the ancient Nile: in flood at certain times, and nearly dry at other times. People's lives here depended on it.

"The dams weren't built until way after the Civil War, and it meant that a lot of land was flooded," Dolly explained. "I expect you know about the old dam here near the marina. There was a ferry landing there, too."

I had heard of the Sumter Ferry and knew there'd been a lock near there before the current one downstream, and nodded.

"What you may not know, is that after that first lock was built, the river level went from just over thirty feet above sea level to forty-one feet. Land was flooded, and the white bluffs were ten feet shorter – when the river was low. The present dam raised the river more than another thirty feet – flooding a lot more land and taking the bluffs to their current height."

I thought about this. It could make Northaw more difficult to find.

"Which dam flooded the Confederate cemetery?"

"The first one," Dolly replied, then gave a sinister giggle. "And, no one knows if the bodies were reburied."

I had heard this, but Dolly's confirmation of the uncertainty surprised me.

"That's like the movie *Poltergeist*!" I exclaimed.

"Well, don't worry, ghosts don't like water much," she replied, with another laugh.

I gave her a serious look and she stopped laughing instantly.

"What is it?"

"In one of our last conversations, Lahoma talked about painting the ceiling under the balcony haint blue," I said.

Dolly returned the serious look.

"I think you'd better tell me everything."

Northaw

7 I was mightily surprised by Master Petey grabbin' me and tryin' to kiss me, but I weren't nearly as surprised as he was to find out who I really was. I didn't know that he didn't know. Of course, he took it out on Peony, shoutin' and stompin' and threatenin' to tell his father.

"Tell him what, chile?" Peony demanded, but in her almost joking tone. "Believe it or not, Master Pierre, I think you'll find he already knows."

Oooh, he were cross. Went all red and stompt up the stairs. Peony smiled at me.

"I don't think you have any more to worry about – from him, at least," an' she laughed all the way back into the kitchen.

It was true enough, too. Pierre François never even talked to me for a long time.

Not til he told me he was goin' to leave Northaw.

The last of the people left the party. Some were taken by Monsieur's hands by boat, while others drove to Glovers Ferry, the way they'd come.

Pierre François' kissin' weren't the only kissin' that night. There was people behind pillars, hedges, in the gardens and behind the quarters and stables. My bad luck to be grabbed by the only person who wasn't supposed to.

I followed Peony into the kitchen where there was plenty to do. Work was relieved by a good amount of the

85

food that was left over, Madame and Monsieur would expect to see the meat, but not the vegetables. We had plenty of them and could produce them new for the table. The fire and stove were boiling water for washing platters, serving dishes, plates, cutlery and all the pots, pans and trays for cooking. It made it very hot, and there were lots of people there, each with a job with Peony shouting at them.

We'd all changed out of our uniforms and hung them safely away from the mess. Some weren't wearing much, but there was no one around to see. The sun would be up soon and we'd jus' have to carry on as though it were a ordinary morning.

In the next few days, it was clear that Madame wanted to know what people thought and were saying about the party. She seemed pleased that so many came, given the river to cross, but the comments given to her when the guests left and the many thank you letters she received did not satisfy as to what people in town were saying. With only about six hundred people living in town, there wouldn't be anyone – 'cept they was dead – that hadn't heard about the Lefever's party.

Her curiosity got the better of her and she went by carriage over the ferry into town. She took Minnie with her who could act as her spy. Minnie was about my age and was the daughter of one of the managers. Her mother had died a few years back and Madame had looked after her a bit.

Sometimes Minnie and I did things together – run around, gather apples and plums, sit with the boys while they fished, and worked in the kitchen, or made beds and swept the house.

Away from the house, Minnie acted like a friend, but near the house, she was a pure white girl. She had ideas about being married to a plantation owner an' livin' in a house "much grander than Northaw," and being the lady who had the best parties in Marengo County.

When she was actin' stuck up, I stayed out of her way, but she'd always eventually come to find me and we'd go hide in the woods by the river, or have some fun with the boys when they weren't workin'.

Anyways, Minnie goes into town with Madame and goes into the shops while Madame waits in the carriage and accepts compliments from passersby. Minnie would come out of the shops with parcels and load them into the carriage and tell Madame what people were sayin' while they drove to the next shop.

Course, this didn't take long, the town being so small, but they went to the Upper Landing to watch a steamboat come in, load and depart.

"That was the best bit," Minnie told me, when she got back to Northaw. "Rufus says there are hundreds of places for steamboats to stop between Columbus and Mobile. I'd like to go up and down the river and get off and visit at each stop."

Rufus was about a hundred years old with a white beard, but he knew horses well and looked good sitting up there drivin' the carriage. He was good with most animals and doctored them, and Monsieur said it was his work with horses that made him famous in three counties. He could break them, train them, deliver them, and drive them.

"An' no one knows how he does it," Jody told me. "He collects herbs and roots for his potions and poultices an' brews 'em up in his quarters. No one sees how he does it.

"When he breaks an' trains a horse, he doesn't mind if people watch, but no one has been able to work out how he does it," Jody said. "He talks to them. He's never rough, and he never looks frightened."

Jody told me about different men tryin' to do what they saw Rufus doin' an' everyone watchin' would fall about laughin' as horses wouldn't do anythin' until Rufus was sent for.

Minnie was pretty, but not as pretty as she thought she was. Not as special, neither. Once she turned sixteen, she didn't want anythin' to do with me. Said that Monsieur treated me better than her which was wrong. We stayed out of each other's way, but I missed her company going for walks, fishin', gatherin' berries and fruit an' sittin' with the boys.

Northaw

We'd still work together in the kitchens and serving upstairs when needed, but she was comin' to hate Northaw.

"It takes too long to get anywhere," she'd complain. "I want to be able to walk into town an' get on a steamboat and go down to Mobile, or up to Tuscaloosa. That's where I'll meet someone rich."

She'd talk this way to upset me. She was always careful not to go too far because she was afraid I'd tell Monsieur, and she'd get into trouble. He might have fathered me, and I think he did look after me and Mam from a distance, but I never talked to him 'cept about what I was doin'. If I had problems, I'd tell Mam or Peony. They knew what I'd be able to do.

"Don't you worry about Miss Minnie," Peony would say. "Her ideas will disappear pretty quick one day."

An' she was right.

Ben's Notes

I knew I could do with Dolly's help, so I started telling her about Lahoma and the things she said. We walked to the old landing where I would meet Lahoma, and we hoped that she might show up.

"Do you think she might be a loose nut?" Dolly asked.

I looked at her questioningly.

"One of those people who got kicked out when all the asylums closed and have to wander around all day."

"I don't think so. If so, she's harmless, and while odd, her talk isn't crazy."

As I tried to describe her, I realized that because she had sat next to me, I had focused far more on what she said than what she looked like. It was like trying to describe someone you saw in a dream.

What she looked like to me was less important than what she said, so I moved the conversation back to what she had told me about. I gave Dolly the names she had used, but apart from Monsieur Lefever (or Lefebvre), there were only first names, and many of those would be the unrecorded names of slaves, as Dolly pointed out.

I told her about the boats and the fishing, the building of the house, the illegitimacy and mixed race of Lahoma, the killings and the weights of cotton bales that she had given me. When I finished, it was apparent to me that although Lahoma's stories were beautifully woven, there was very little substance to them.

When I finished, Dolly stared at me with a totally blank expression.

"Ben, you're very nice, but the words 'Shaggy Dog' come to mind," she finally said.

I nodded.

"And, you're not doing drugs?"

I smiled.

"No."

"Okay, there's only one name that you've given me that might be traceable, but you should know that one of the main founders of Demopolis was General Charles Lefebvre-Desnouettes, or Count Desnouettes."

This rang a bell from schoolsdays.

Northaw

"Did he have a son – brother, nephew? Henri Jacques was much younger. Probably born around 1800. Maybe in this country."

"Well that gives us something to start with," Dolly said, undaunted. "You've got the son's name, too."

I nodded.

"And did she say where they lived?"

I thought this was the big one. In my head, it was sort of the make-or-break piece. If it existed, then its story would be known, and Lahoma would likely be – who knows? A con artist? If it wasn't real – well, the result would be the same.

There was nothing for it.

"As near as I can tell, it was across the river in the southern part of what is now Daub's Swamp, west – that's down stream – of Glover's Ferry," I said. "The plantation was called Northaw."

Surprisingly, this got very little reaction from Dolly. She nodded and thought.

Suddenly, she started, looked at her watch and stood up.

"I'm sorry, Ben. I must go," she said. "My parents are having people around and I said I'd help my mother."

I stood, too.

She fished in her bag and drew out a bent business card.

"Come to my house tomorrow at ten," she said. "You've given me a lot to think about."

Then, very briefly, she slipped her arm around me, kissed my cheek, and rushed off.

☙

It was a beautiful morning when I set off down to Dolly's house on a road to the south of town called The Cove. Houses there cost about what a block of buildings would cost in town, and, to my way of thinking, they weren't very attractive. The road followed the old Whitfield Canal, dug by slaves as a drainage ditch to prevent Whitfield's plantation, Gaineswood, from flooding before the dams. The ebb and flow of the Tombigbee would radically alter the nature of a canal from a dry gulch to a deep and flowing channel.

The construction of the dams, as Dolly had observed, raised the water levels by at least forty feet and altered the shape of the dry land.

I found the Madison's house, an attractive one-story brick house with three dormer windows. It had a well tended lawn and enough mature trees to make it look like it had been there a lot longer than it had.

Dolly opened the door and led me to the back of the house and into the back yard and down its lawn towards the canal.

"Where are we going?"

"If you want to find Northaw, you'd better know what you're looking for."

We rounded a clump of rhododendron and there was a slip cut into the garden with a wooden dock. Nestling in it was a small cabin cruiser. It had the look of a vintage Chris-Craft with the dark wood cabin, but with a fiberglass hull. The wheel was undercover and open to the stern with places for chairs and a table, and there was what looked like a decent sized cabin.

"My father insisted on calling her *Dolly*," she said. "I always call it the *Dollybird* because I did so many stupid things on it when I was in high school and college."

I laughed.

She gestured to me to cast off.

"Wild child?"

As she was preparing to start the engine, I climbed aboard.

"When you know you're going to be married off to someone respectable and have to host charity events and church fairs for the rest of your life, a girl needs a few embarrassing memories."

We laughed, and she expertly backed the boat into the canal and headed to the river.

I sat next to her as she steered.

"I have spent hours exploring streams and inlets," she said. "I have looked for some of the old farms and homesteads, too. So, I'm going to show you a few of the ones I found and identified."

In a few minutes we joined the river and headed up stream.

"In the steamboat days with no communication, coming into the curves, the boats would give one blast on the whistle if they were coming down on the right side – heading south – or two, if they were on the left.

"During the day, you could see the smoke, but even then, you didn't know what side they were on."

"Weren't there rules?"

"Not really," she said. "Boats had to follow the deepest part of the river and avoid underwater snags and overhanging branches. Remember, when the river rose, the branches were much lower.

"Bars of sand and silt would form on curves and force the steamboats to whichever side they needed to be on to avoid them," she continued. "Also, it was not unusual for bends to be so tight that the boats needed to reverse from a bank in order to get around them – like trying to turn a car around on a very narrow road."

Even going twice as fast as a steamboat would have gone, life slowed right down on this modern boat.

"This looks like a conventional boat," Dolly said, "but it has a double hull like a catamaran, so its draft is very shallow. It does mean that if a large barge goes by, it feels like very rough seas."

She smiled at me and laughed.

We made our way along the bluffs and up towards the marina.

"Before any of the dams, these bluffs were eighty feet or more," she said.

"I did grow up here, Dolly," I said. "I know I look dumb and talk to lunatics, but I'm not totally stupid."

I didn't know how she'd react, but she burst out laughing and apologized.

"All right," she said. "I'll assume that you know things if you promise to ask if you don't."

"Fine," I said, and she smiled.

We passed the entrance to the marina. There was no traffic which I remarked on.

"We're between the early fishermen, and those who wait until after lunch," she joked.

After a few minutes she said:

"Okay, you know that inlet," she said.

"Culpepper Slough."

"Right, now, we're going to head up the next little inlet before the river."

"I didn't know there was one," I said.

She swung the boat toward the middle of the river then hooked back downstream.

"Look," she said. "There's a small peninsula of trees and an inlet. Most people never notice it."

It was no more than about twenty feet wide, and Dolly cut the speed, and we crawled in.

It's very like Culpepper Slough," she explained. "There's the narrow entrance and then – well, just wait."

We turned out from the narrow channel and a lake, nearly a mile long, opened before us. It had a surface like a mirror and was tree-lined down to the water's edge.

"How deep is this?" I asked.

"Hard to tell. You'd have to know what it was like before it was flooded – or flooded more. There are maps, but I've never looked."

"Ever swum here?" I asked.

"Don't," she said, in a warning tone. "As we head to the other end, watch for ripples on the surface – like that one! – or that one!"

"Alligators," I said, chastened.

"See you later," she said, and smiled.

Northaw

8 I wonder who this Indian girl is that Ben's been seeing? I don't think she's Choctaw. Chickasaw or Creek, maybe. Blood's pretty watered down, so it's hard to tell.

I don't think anything really bad happened to Minnie, not like to some of us, but that didn't mean that she *wasn't* hugely disappointed with her life. Not unexpectedly – given her activities and determination to find a husband and escape Demopolis – Minnie found she was going to have a baby. She was sixteen. She told the boy she thought would give her the best chance at runnin' away and makin' her dreams. Will Briar was a nice boy, but he was only fourteen an' panicked, told his parents, and they disappeared on the next steamboat headin' south.

Her father might have caught them and dragged Will back, but she didn't tell him.

Still, Minnie wasn't put off. There were a number of boys to choose from. John Gilbert simply said she was out of her mind an' everyone knew it, and that she'd have to find "some other sucker."

So, she did.

She married Beau Bloomer. He was fifteen and a nice boy, too. When you're a slave and someone's nice to you, you 'preciate it. Beau wasn't very bright, and he may or may not have been the father, but since he didn't rightly remember what happened in the orchard when she'd

101

turned up with some corn whiskey that had jus' been made, he agreed. No one was delighted, but no one was too upset, neither – 'cept Minnie.

She almost got her dream. Her daughter was very pretty and when she turned seventeen, she married Simon, son of John Gilbert, who could have been her cousin. It didn't matter because soon after, Simon and his father were killed at Shiloh.

Minnie never left Demopolis. She might be here still.

When you have to go where you're told, you can end up in some strange places and with stranger people. As I said, I been lucky, but you realize that a pet dog is freer than you are.

Who's that girl you're seeing? She's not one of you.

Life might not have been free, but it weren't bad compared to some stories. The earth was fertile, things moved in a steady rhythm – I could see that as I grew older. There still wasn't much here, only a few hundred people, most were on the plantations and farms, but I get to join people on some of the days that the steamships arrived. Sometimes markets were set up right there where the goods were unloaded.

Later, the steamers would stop at Webb's to load cotton then stop here to unload food and goods. Or the other way round dependin' if they was going up or down river.

Northaw

There was a cotton gin here by then. Minnie's husband worked at it. Monsieur wanted to get his own, but it would need more slaves, and the land was too low to risk other people's cotton if there were flooding.

Maybe a year or two after the party, people started talkin' about Madame Lefever actin' strange-like. She didn't drink – we all knew that – but she'd see things, talk to people who weren't there an' sometimes throw things off the balcony near the bedroom door. Then she'd sleep. Seeming for days.

The doctor came and gave her medicine. Peony didn't think much of it, and neither did Mam. Mam called her high-strung – and Peony didn't think much of the doctor.

"Rufus says he wouldn't let that man treat a sick horse, let alone one of the leading ladies of the South!"

'Part from that, nothin' much changed. Pierre François was a little more loose about his comings and goings, and Monsieur always looked worried. He was still nice to people and made sure things were done right, but talk was that there were troubles comin'.

Monsieur and a number o' men – white men only, so we knew it wasn't plantation business – would read newspapers that came from Mobile and sometimes Norleans an' shake their heads.

I talked to Jody about what they might be sayin' as I'd never seen the men like that, but Jody didn't know either, but said it must be bad as no one else seemed to know.

The summer I was about eighteen, the water in the rivers was so low that it was possible to walk to Demopolis. Our feet and hems would be wet when we got there, but Jody an' I went with the men. They were taking some slaves down to Mobile to sell. The water was only two feet deep and in many places it was dry. At one time rock and gravel had been laid to make a ford. Bits had washed away, and it was easier and less muddy. Where the crossing was it was only a few hundred feet to the other side. This made it faster to walk the mile and a half to the Upper Landing.

I'll never forget the look of the slaves as they moved along in the coffle. They looked really sad and scared, shufflin' along slow. They seemed to know that where they went next probly wouldn't be as good a place to be.

I didn't know them, but they was never chained up at Northaw. They were fairly new slaves, bought last year to help with digging a new bed for the stream that would give another few acres for cotton without having to cross it.

Jody had heard Rufus say that Monsieur wanted to keep the slaves to help farm the land and do building work with Jonah to gussy up the plantation so it looked more like some of the grand houses that was being built.

'Parently, Monsieur said he was sellin' 'em 'cos of the low cotton price, but I heard Mam tell Peony that it was because the river was low and that was making food, cloth, and all goods more expensive.

Northaw

Peony thought it was more serious than that. She used a few big words I didn't know but said it would turn the world upside down.

Who knew what that meant?

Well, I guess the slaves bein' sold did. They were good lookin', strong young men. Two of them were Choctaw, too. To me, that meant that even Mam could be sold and that made me scared.

That would really turn the world upside down.

Ben's Notes

"What a place to dump a body!" I exclaimed, before I had the chance to think of how it would sound to Dolly.

Maybe it would make her feel unsafe with me. Then I thought, maybe it's me who should feel unsafe.

Dolly's laughter told me there was nothing to worry about.

"I bring all my new boyfriends here just to let them know they shouldn't mess with me," she said. "It is beautiful, isn't it?"

At that moment, so was Dolly.

I could see I'd have to be careful as I had no intention to stop traveling and live in Demopolis.

We were moving very slowly.

"I don't come here that often and who knows what's in the water," she said. "During dry spells, people have found stolen cars on the bottom. Keep an eye out."

The water was still and dark, though looking straight down, it was more clear than any water I'd seen around here.

"You should have a line for soundings," I said.

"I think that every time I come here, but somehow never remember," she replied. "See those oak trees? That's our first stop."

We crawled towards it, and Dolly ran the boat up the muddy bank.

"Take the line and tie it to something," she said. "Try not to jump into the silt or I'll have to use the boat to pull you out."

I laughed.

"It would look like you were fishing for alligators," I replied.

"You understand. Good."

I secured the boat to a small tree. It didn't need to be strong as the boat was light and there was little discernible current. I threw a small stick into the water to see if it moved at all.

It did in an inexorable way but at a speed of only a few feet per minute.

I gave Dolly a hand down from the boat. Her grip was strong, and her hand rougher than I'd expected, and I wondered what she did. Gardening? Brick laying? Grave digging?

"This is lesson one in recognizing old homesteads," she said, in a mock-lecturing way.

"Before we explore, tell me why you think I looked here in the first place."

I liked this. She was thinking like a historian.

"Old maps. Old stories. Someone told you," I ventured.

"All possibilities. In this case, I did see something on a map that made me look here, but once I saw the place, there were other clues."

It was just woods. No walls, no chimneys, no foundations? No sign of a landing.

I looked at her.

"What did I tell you to look for when I pointed to the land?"

Got it.

"Oak trees."

She smiled.

"These don't go back to the Civil War, but they grew from acorns that did. Everything else around is fast-growing pine, beech, cottonwoods, river birch, sycamore," she said. "Sycamores, for example, are dirty trees, always shedding something, so people don't like them close to their houses, and there aren't any here."

We walked into the woods. There was no path, but low underbrush and ferns where we walked.

"Now, there – pecans, black walnut, dogwood and magnolia – those are something you'd want close to your house," she explained. "Cedar trees, too. Dead giveaway."

She scanned the ground.

"In the spring, signs of bulb flowers are good indicators of a homestead," she continued. "When I've been here in the spring, there are daffodils and tulips."

We moved further into the woods, and she pointed to a hillock covered with ivy.

"Pull some of the ivy back," she said, and just when I had my hand in it, she added, "and watch out for cotton mouths."

I pulled my hand back quickly but tore out several vines.

"You are trying to kill me!" I exclaimed, laughing.

"Not yet. I need you to push the boat out."

We laughed, then she pointed to the small area that had been uncovered.

"What do you see?"

I stared into the shadowy area.

"Bricks," I said, amazed.

"It's a chimney pile," Dolly said.

I stepped back to take a look at it.

Northaw

It was impossible to imagine anything civilized here.

"Have you been here in winter when the vegetation is down?" I asked.

"It's still pretty overgrown, but I was able to find what I think was a foundation pillar," she said. "Maybe two. There's some broken glass and pottery, and some square-head nails."

I looked up.

"Square-heads are usually pre-1880 and handmade," she said.

"Do you know who owned it or anything?"

"There was a family named Dodge who owned the land in 1875, but that doesn't mean they lived here. They could have been tenants. Could have been former slaves. The map just has the land but no indication of buildings."

She began moving back towards the boat.

"You can get sucked into this stuff for weeks," she said. "The records are good, but they don't answer all the questions," she said. "Come. I'm hungry."

I untied the boat and held onto the line until I was aboard. Dolly backed it out a way then turned very slowly. It was very shallow, and I stayed on the small forward deck and scanned for roots and rocks.

"I'd love to know how deep this is," I said.

"We can do soundings one day if you stick around," she said.

"You make it sound so exciting."

"It's not one of the things that interests me," she said.

"Your blog is more about people," I said.

"You've read it," she said, smiling. "You write about towns, factories and the businesses – the trades – that made them. Things."

"Things are more cooperative," I said.

She turned the boat so that it faced towards the furthest point and switched off the engine.

"I'll get lunch."

She went into the cabin and came back with a picnic basket. I unfolded some chairs that she pointed to and put them on the back deck.

"Aren't you going to drop anchor?"

"We won't drift far."

She put the basket on a small table, and I looked eagerly inside, missing the view of her removing her shirt to reveal a bikini top. The sun was warm, but I didn't think that warm.

During the half hour we ate, the silence settled on us. It was almost as profound as in the desert.

She stowed the picnic basket when we finished, and I folded the chairs and table and secured them. Dolly returned to the helm and started the engine. The boat had barely moved, though we'd turned about a hundred degrees like a compass needle.

"Now, I want you to scan the shoreline," she said as we got underway and on the right heading. "You know what to look for now."

The boat glided along at a walking pace. I watched the shore and then it clicked.

"You know where there is one and you're making me focus my brain and eyes!"

I looked through the windshield at her and saw her big smile.

We might have gone a few hundred yards, and I saw it.

"Stop the boat!" I shouted. "No, turn here!"

I pointed and climbed back into the cabin expecting to see a look of approving satisfaction, but she looked puzzled. She turned the boat, took a pair of binoculars from a compartment, and walked to the rear deck.

"I'll be damned," she whispered. "I thought I'd found them all. Let's see what we've got."

Northaw

9 Once the steamboat pulled in, I understood why so many of us had gone with the slaves: it was to carry things back to Northaw. The slaves were on the main deck and sat on or around the cotton bales, animal pens and cargo. Unless you were on the side away from the sun, it could be uncomfortable, according to Jonah.

You'd be in the sun, or against the wall next to the boiler. In the winter, that was fine, but in August it was terrible. This was June, so it weren't too bad. The white men went upstairs to the cabin on the boiler deck and spent time in the cabin where there was a bar and maybe food. They drank, played cards and smoked all the way to Mobile. 'Least that was the 'speclation as Peony called it.

We said goodbye to the men and the slaves, and watched the smoke get thicker, jumped when we heard the whistle and stepped back when the great wheel began to turn to back the boat away from the bank then head down the river. We watched it until it was out of sight – which was pretty soon because of the bend, though the smoke was visible for a lot longer.

We gathered our peach baskets, sacks of vegetables, boxes of biscuits, and some dress material and lace for Madame, and made our way back.

It didn't seem to take that long on the way back, but the carrying was awkward. We swapped what we carried a few times just so it didn't seem we'd carried it that far.

I drank a jug of cold water when I got back to the house, then went out in the orchard and lay on the grass in the shade with Jody.

I couldn't stop thinkin' about the men on their trip down river not knowin' what would come next.

I wondered why Minnie wanted to go.

ଓ

Ben wants me to say more about the house. He was interested in walking across the river and asked questions about the ford, like was it possible to drive a wagon across? That made me laugh. He's clearly never seen the bottom of the Black Warrior.

I don't know what much more I can say.

Jody and Jonah used to talk about it all the time. I don't know why Ben asks as he can just look at it, but he says he doesn't know where it is. I already told him about the brick pillars that were whitewashed. There were six across the front and down the sides.

The house was square forty feet by forty feet. Upstairs there was a balcony around three sides that was five feet wide. One day when I was workin' up there, Jody came up and lay down across the balcony and said it was five feet. Ben said that meant that the pillars would have been about fifty feet across depending where it was measured from.

Originally, the house was going to be square, but they decided to make space for a bigger kitchen and bedrooms for the household slaves attached to the back of the house

Northaw

with the kitchen in case they were needed during the night. Some of them was upstairs, but they would have to use the indoor stairs which kept them apart from the master's rooms.

At first, there was a broad wooden staircase to the upper floor from the outside. It had what Monsieur called a gracious slope, but someone at the party remarked that it was rather plain and talked about the double curved ones they'd seen somewheres.

That made up Madame's mind, even though guests would seldom go to the upper floor, and if they did, it would be from the inside. It didn't matter, so Jonah and two other slaves spent half the summer building it. Everyone wanted to do it in wood, but Madame wanted it in brick cemented to look like stone, which took twice as long to build, and as Monsieur said, you couldn't hear anyone come up it.

Peony made us laugh saying that Madame wouldn't mind being murdered as long as the killer was impressed with the staircase to her bedroom.

Downstairs, there was Monsieur's office which Madame always called a "library" even though it hardly had any books, a dining room, a party room and a morning room that could open into the party room. There was a dark wood staircase to upstairs, and at the back a door into the extension where the kitchen was, a place for household slaves to eat, and three bedrooms above, under an unfinished pitched roof.

One room, the biggest, was for the men, one was for Mam and me, and one was for the women – Peony and the maids, includin' Peony's assistant, a very stupid girl who could barely peel potatoes.

I almost never saw the bedrooms, though I cleaned the upstairs hallway and balconies. Only two maids were allowed in the bedrooms. They each had two bedrooms assigned, but decided themselves that it was easier, faster and more fun to do all the rooms t'gether.

I think Monsieur knew, and Pierre François didn't care.

There were no rooms in the attic and no windows. The roof was a shallow pitch and there were four chimneys plus the one in the kitchen where there was a cast iron stove and fireplace.

I don't know if the furniture was good, or anything else they had.

All I know is that Madame said it wasn't.

Ben asked about floors. Upstairs, they were wood of course. They were waxed and polished and there were rugs.

Downstairs was the same 'cept for Monsieur's office where there was painted stretched canvas. I had to brush it on my knees.

The kitchen had a brick floor and the porches around the ground floor were brick and on ground level but down two steps from the main floor in case of flooding. The kitchen wasn't up two steps which made wheeling barrows of wood, fruit and vegetables in easy. I said I guessed it didn't matter if it flooded.

Peony said it would matter when the fire went out and Madame had to eat raw catfish.

Ben's Notes

I was trying not to be smug about finding a homestead – maybe a plantation – that Dolly didn't know about. I could be wrong, but the closer we got to the shore, the more promising I thought it looked.

That was until an alligator slithered into the water with a splash from the bank we were headed for.

Dolly cut the engine and let the boat drift into the mud. It was far enough in that we could jump on the grass without getting wet or filthy. She went into the cabin again, I thought perhaps to use the head, but when she emerged, she had put on a cotton shirt and was holding a revolver in one hand and a machete in the other. That took me straight back to my comment about good places to dump bodies.

She joined me on the foredeck and handed me the machete.

"Take the line, jump over, pull the boat in as far as you can and tie it off. I'll watch for gators."

Her orders were clear, but jumping off a boat with a machete was new to me. Still, I was able to do all those things without having my leg bitten off, being shot or falling on the blade. Once steady, I held out my hand to Dolly. She tucked the revolver under the belt at the back of her jeans, took my hand and jumped down.

"My father insists I take the gun when I go on my excursions," she said. "It scares the hell out of new boyfriends, and they behave, more's the pity."

"Probably why your father makes you bring it."

She looked at me from the corner of her eye and smiled.

"Let's see what we've got."

We walked to the oak I'd seen, and then saw several others, extending in a line.

"An avenue?" I asked.

She kept her focus on the larger trees.

"Maybe. They could be border oaks," she glanced at me to see if I understood. I shook my head.

"It was an English custom to plant oaks along the border of your property if you had a good sized estate. Maybe the French did, too," she explained. "You agreed the line with your neighbor, and they were planted in his presence. In a few places, the trees alternate, defining the boundary as the line that ran between the trees."

Northaw

We didn't go too far in immediately. Dolly was listening – for what I didn't know. Alligators? Snakes? Bears?

For all its beauty, this was a land for missing people.

I decided to tell Dolly a little more about Northaw as it doubled the chances of the story surviving if I did not. She listened with interest but made no comment, then returned to our present exploration.

"This is promising," Dolly said, stirring me from my *memento mori*. "Look – dogwood, apple and pear trees."

We moved further into the woods, and I slashed at some undergrowth.

"Would there have been roads to these places?"

"This is part of Webb's Bend – which you know; there would have been a network of lanes and paths," she said, holding a branch back for me to pass. "Kingfisher Road, which ran down to Lock 4, and the roads to Glover's Ferry would have connected to any farms here.

"Also, you forget that there may have been roads that are now underwater," she added, pointing to the lake. "Think what that area would look like if you dropped the water level by fifty feet."

I thought about this.

"So, any buildings here may have been on a hill set well back from the road?" I mused. "That's quite a thought."

She nodded, then stopped to look for any indications of settlement, then looked at me.

"Not bad, Choctaw. The old maps don't help a lot," she explained. "They show who owned the land but not any buildings, and because the land was leased out, there's no record of who or what was here."

She stopped and thought for a moment.

"I've not tried this, but if you could locate the papers of the old owners, they might contain records of the rents paid and you could piece it together from that."

I nodded.

"Good detective work," I said, "but in the case of Northaw, I'm making an assumption that it was part of the original Vine and Olive purchase that was still in the Lefebvre family."

She considered this, then shook her head.

"That land was a good way east of town. There's a marker on Route 80 near the cement works' entrance."

"I knew a historian would be useful to have along," I said, and she smiled.

She went back to studying our surroundings.

"Now, what have we got here?"

There was a large heap of vines, out of which rose the base of a broad, brick chimney, rising to about seven feet.

Unafraid of snakes, Dolly picked up a piece of branch and, after breaking off excess twigs, had fashioned a hook-like tool and began pulling vines from where we expected to find the fireplace.

"That's very broad," I said, looking at the result.

"There may have been iron racks for cooking, grilling, drying and other tasks done by brick ovens. These were easier to build, but it did alter the type of cooking you could do."

She stopped to think.

"Houses here would have been good for slave accommodation," she said. "It's bounded by the river and the state road, which would have had regular traffic. There would be very little place for them to go."

We thought about that.

"The Indian slaves could have headed back to their tribes," I suggested.

"If they were still in the area," Dolly countered. "Many had been moved on, and it's unlikely that the slaves knew that."

"It's almost impossible to imagine," I said. "There's only oral tradition to rely on."

Dolly gave one of her laughs.

"And how much Choctaw history came to you via your family?" she challenged.

"None," I admitted. "We never talked much about being part Choctaw – I mean, we knew we were, but I don't think I knew any more about Choctaw culture than my Scottish-American classmates did about theirs."

"Same with me," Dolly said. "Like your Scots friends, all we knew were the stereotypes and caricatures."

"And what we were taught at school."

"There's the irony," she said, laughing again.

She started back to the boat.

"I'll put this one on my map," she said, saving the GPS coordinates on her phone. "I was going to go down to the far end and show you another one I found, but it's not as good as this one. Would you like to come back one day and try mapping it when we've brought all the right stuff?"

Like a shovel for burying bodies?

"Sure! That would be great."

"I know it's early, but let's go to the old landing and see if Lahoma will join us," Dolly said.

It was time to start getting some answers, so I agreed.

When we reached the boat, I untied it and helped Dolly aboard – a token, I know, as she was very capable – and clambered in after giving it a push.

"I need to stow the gun and use the head," she said, disappearing into the cabin. "Take us out!"

I'd driven boats before on my travels, and this was like most. I wasn't sure how much power I'd need to get off the bank and may have overdone it for a few seconds, but it worked.

I pointed us towards the access to the river, watching for logs, alligators, mines and sudden attacks from behind.

Northaw

10

I saw Ben and the woman sittin' on the bank thinking about the steamers that used to land there, but it weren't nothin' like that. I didn't want to talk to the woman. She was the wrong mixup. Not French. Not Choctaw. Looked like she'd be as bossy as Madame, too. At least she was sittin' to Ben's left. I sat on his right so I wouldn't have to talk to her.

"Hey, Ben," I said, an' sat next to him.

"Hey, Lahoma. I want you to meet Dolly."

Dolly leaned forwards to see me and said, "Hey." She didn't try to shake hands or nothin', an' she let Ben do the talkin', so it was like befores.

Our talks are nice. A few words of greetin' an' then Ben asks a question. It's almost always one I can answer. Sometimes, I can tell from his look that he wants more, but it's up to me whether I give him more. Jody could be like that. Jody says that questions are like keys that open doors.

"Sometimes, you know what's behind the door, so you don't open it. Sometimes, it's the wrong key and nothing opens."

Ben seems to know this too. I might tell him about the keys one day.

Today, Ben asks where the slaves lived at Northaw. I can open that door. He already knows about Mam and me, and Peony and the house slaves, but field slaves and the buildin' slaves live between the house and the cotton fields.

129

There are six houses, some bigger than others. Building slaves – the ones that worked with wood and sometimes stone or bricks – were in a house that looked large, but more than half of it was the wood shop. They did everything from planting trees and cuttin' down, sawing planks unless there were ones that needed to go to the sawmill. They could make tools and bits of furniture. There were always a few boys there bein' trained.

There were three cotton houses – two for men, one for women. The women worked with the cotton gin as well as in the fields. Some of them thought they were special but if the managers found out, they'd be punished – or worse, the manager would ask Rufus or Badger to make sure they behaved.

Then there were two tobacco houses. Northaw didn't grow much tobacco, but Monsieur learned some tricks about curing and used 'em here.

"If we can send fine tobacco ready to be used to Europe we can be paid more and they can sell it more cheaply we'll do well."

There were five or six plantation owners who set up a cigar business together. The wrapin' leaf came from up North somewheres, but the rest was from right along the river on plantations from here to Coffeeville.

The men were always takin' about the cigar women on the Coffeeville plantation and down in Cuba. They were supposed to be special somehow. These cigars were supposed to be special, too. Monsieur liked them and would smoke them only once a week an' on special occasions an' hand 'em out like special presents to guests and people he wanted to do business with.

That was another thing – every year, each of the six plantations would supply a large cedar log for makin' boxes for the cigars.

I started laughin', and Ben asked me what was funny. I told him I just remembered that they used to make cheap cigars from the tailin's and waste from the good ones. They were made last and each plantation owner got boxes of them. How many they got depended on things like how much tobacco they supplied and how much cedar.

"They're not great, but better than most," Monsieur said. "Good for handing around at card games and on steamboats."

Thinking of Monsieur saying this always made me laugh. The slaves smoked this tobacco, too, or chewed it. Chewin' was most common, but they'd make pipes an' some made cigars, but not always of tobacco leaves. Dependin' on the time of year, corn husks were often used, but as Jody and I found out one afternoon, it was terrible.

Ben's friend giggled at this and tried to hide it. Strange girl.

She whispered something to Ben. He nodded, but didn't say anything.

I went on tellin' him about tobacco and the slave quarters, and Ben listened. Sometimes, he'd scribble things down when I talked. He would bring me the pages he'd written and read them to me. He usually got it right, but sometimes I didn't remember tellin' him things. Also, when he changed the order around, it wasn't as easy for me to remember.

I had stopped to think, and the girl said some more things to him. I never used to say things that people thought was rude, but I didn't like her.

"Why do you listen to her, Ben? She's Creek – or more like Alabama, not like you and me. Be careful, Ben."

Sometimes I'd talk to Jody like that, but I'd never talk like that to a white person. Uppity Creek probably don't realize she's from slaves just like Ben and me.

I didn't say this while the girl was here, but later when I saw Ben on his own. I spose he'll jus' have to learn the hard way.

○ʒ

As time went on and people got better at farming, and the land got used to having to work, Northaw was a busy plantation. There were about thirty of us slaves there – unlike Gaineswood where Mr. Whitfield had more than two hundred – but that was a much bigger plantation. I heard it said that Gaineswood did ten thousand bales per year. At Northaw, we did about a thousand, more or less, but we had the tobacco and fruit and vegetables, too.

That's how Monsieur was able to keep buildin' – for a while at least.

I wonder if *she* knows what I'm talkin' about. Surprised she's not wearing gloves like Madame always used to – even when she stepped out on the balcony outside her bedroom. Sometime the maids would joke about it in the kitchen. Peony might say:

"Prissy, go fetch them chickens I hung this morning and get to pluckin'." And Prissy would say, "Yes, Miss Poeny, as soon as I put my gloves on!"

We'd all laugh, and Peony would pretend to be angry and threaten to whip her, to which Prissy would sass back, "As long as you put *your* gloves on first!"

I only thought this as I was sittin' there with Ben and the Creek, and I laughed, then started giggling an' couldn't stop. The Creek must have thought I was as daft as she was.

Later, when I told Ben what I thought, he laughed hard, too.

Ben's Notes

"She really didn't like me," Dolly said.

"I'm not going to make excuses for her. Did you learn anything?"

"Not a lot of people know how slave quarters were organized," she said. "Probably any combination you can think of was true of some plantations, but this rang true for one of its size. She was right about Gaineswood and Whitfield, too."

"And was she right about the Creeks and Choctaw?" I asked. "Perhaps I should be ashamed that I don't know."

Dolly laughed and gave my arm a light punch.

"I think they had their ups and downs, but I like you well enough," she said.

I waited a moment, enjoying the feeling of connection. Dolly remained quiet, too. Eventually, I spoke.

"So, what did you make of her?"

"Damned if I know," she said. "She looks normal enough. Her country dress could be from any era – and I dare say you could buy one on Washington Street today."

Dolly thought for a moment.

"If you're going to be serious about finding out about Northaw, meet me for a late breakfast at the diner," she instructed. "Bring your notes and I'll bring what I find. I have to see if I can track that ruin you found, too! That could be exciting."

We stood up and brushed the grass from our clothes. Dolly headed to her car and I went home to my small apartment in an old clapboard house on Jackson Street. It was certainly nowhere like Dolly's family house on The Cove.

༜

That evening, I pulled together the "facts" that Lahoma had given me and sorted them into several categories: people, Northaw, Demopolis, the river, and so on.

Thinking about them as I read, I realized how much of what she told me I didn't know or had forgotten. Dolly would be pleased that there were things to check, but I sensed that, like me, what she really wanted to know was, had Northaw existed and if so, where?

༜

As planned, I met Dolly at the diner at ten-thirty. She was more subdued than when I'd left her but made an effort to be cheerful.

When she ordered only toast and coffee, I asked if she was all right.

"Not in trouble for borrowing the boat, are you?" I asked.

She smiled.

"No, that's not it," she said, still smiling. "I've been thinking – brooding, really – about yesterday."

"Did Lahoma upset you that much?" I asked, though I wanted to steer clear of emotional territory.

She shook her head, unconvincingly.

"It was the whole day," she said.

I put my coffee down.

"I thought it was a wonderful day!" I exclaimed. "From the boat ride, the ruins, the lunch, you pulling out a revolver and the encounter with Lahoma. Yeah, she's odd, but what upset you?"

Her coffee came, but she just stared at it.

Finally, she looked up.

"It was fun, but was any of it real?"

"What do you mean?" I asked, delaying getting stuck into my corned beef hash and hash browns.

"When I got home, I was as excited as you, but as I ran though the references I've got and checked old maps, lists of families, and so on, I could find nothing.

"There were Lefebvres, of course, but none of the names you gave me," she said, obviously bruised by the fact she couldn't find these things. "I've got a pretty good map of where the lake we were on was. As you observed, the river – a stream at best – would have been several hundred feet from the ruins we looked at, but there is no sign of the ruin you found on the map. The other two are there, but they are the only ones that side of the lake."

"Any names?"

"The usual ones found around here. Ward and Jackson."

I considered this.

"I don't see that means anything," I said. "It just suggests it wasn't a residence, but an outbuilding of some sort."

"That fireplace was huge."

"A forge, maybe – or a separate bake house or smoke house?"

She thought.

Northaw

"Could have been, I suppose," she conceded. "But that's not the only thing."

I waited while she drank her coffee – which I took as permission to begin my breakfast.

"From what you told me and what Lahoma said, Northaw was on the land that's now Daub's Swamp, north of Webb's Bend and west of Glover's Ferry."

"Exactly," I said.

"According to my 1850 map, that land, about twelve-hundred acres, belonged to none other than Francis Strother Lyon."

It was a name to reckon with. The Lyons had two of the largest houses in Demopolis – and both were still standing. F.S. had been in the United States Congress and later in the Confederate Congress. His home was Bluff Hall and his nephew – a major slave owner – built Lyon Hall.

Lahoma's veracity looked dubious. I said as much to Dolly.

She shrugged.

"I made the biggest mistake of a historian," she said, deflated. "I *wanted* to believe her. I lost my objectivity."

She ate her toast in a desultory fashion and turned her coffee cup with a finger, clockwise, then back, and clockwise again.

"Dolly," I began. "I've been keeping this to myself, but I have been playing with the idea of writing a sort of historical novel about Lahoma and what she's told me.

"I haven't attempted anything like this before, so it might not work," I continued. "So, to some extent, the absolute historical truth is not as critical for that project, but I will share your skepticism in all other approaches to this. Does that make sense?"

"I think so," she said, after thinking about it. "I like the idea. I certainly couldn't do a historical article on what we've got."

"That's it, Dolly," I said. "With fiction, I can write things that historians could only posit."

"Like?" she asked, intrigued.

"The land," I said. "We may never know if Lefebvre ever owned it.

"The 1840s were pretty rough economically, prices were all over the place for cotton, there was already a lot of talk about ending slavery, and shipping and selling cotton was dependent on the state of the river," I continued, and Dolly nodded.

"Suppose – and I don't think we'll ever find evidence for this – suppose Lefebvre sold the land to Lyon but held a lease on it?"

Dolly shook her head.

"So he had to pay to use land that he could use for nothing before?" she asked.

"Yes, but he'd have a lump sum that could keep the plantation running, perhaps for decades."

She nodded.

"Big risk."

"Maybe he saw the end coming."

Dolly thought a while longer.

"It's plausible, but I'm not convinced," she said. "Shall we see what we can find at the library and historical society?"

Northaw

11 Sometimes it seemed like Peony held Northaw together. No one knew much about her, but everyone thought she was a good cook, and she ran the kitchen well. Monsieur treated her well – she even had her own bedroom (the silly girl was now workin' in the fields), tiny, but her own, while Mam and I shared. Sometimes, if visitors brought maids with them, we'd have to share with them, too.

Sometimes those maids thought they were as good as their mistresses. They'd come down to the kitchen an' 'spect to be waited on. Pinchin' food, or acting fancy with the household men. Peony made sure they behaved.

One day she caught a visitin' maid liftin' an apple from the larder. Grabbed her by the ear and dragged her out of the kitchen and locked her in the fruit cellar. That was one place I didn't want to go alone. The swamp was less scaresome.

It was underground with a great mound of earth on top with wooden stairs goin' down to the door. It was on the highest ground near the house so it wouldn't flood and were wonderful cool in the summer. Inside, it was dark and almost silent. Jonah once said it was like a grave, and that's all I could think about when I was down there.

Around lunch time, Monsieur comes into the kitchen askin' where the maid was, as her mistress was gettin' ready to come down to eat and needed help washin' or dressin'.

Peony was so brave – very polite – but very brave. She walked right up Monsieur and told him:

"I caught that pretty missy from Eutaw stealin' one of your apples an' I put her in the fruit cellar," she declared, as loudly as a steamboat captain.

Monsieur took time to think about this. With anyone else he would have exploded instantly. He seemed to swell up and we all thought he would just blow up, but then he deflated and when he spoke, spoke gently.

"You protected my apples, did you, Peony?" he asked. "Well, locking someone in the fruit cellar is a bad thing to do, but so is stealing my apples."

He motioned for her to follow him, and we all looked out the door and watched them go to the fruit cellar. Peony went down the stairs while Monsieur waited at the top, an' we began to hear screamin' and shoutin' an' saw the maid come up the stairs.

When she first come up, she looked as white as Monsieur, then turned red in fury, but she went white again as soon as she saw Monsieur and stopped screamin' and movin'.

There was three of four of us in the doorway watchin' and tryin' to listen, but we couldn't hear anything. Peony comes back to the kitchen door and Monsieur takes the girl into the house through the front door. We all rush to the door to the hallway that leads to the dining room, but we can't hear anything because they've shut the big doors.

Northaw

We turn to get back to work in the kitchen when we hear a cry and steps running towards us.

The maid rushes passed us to the outside door and outside. We race across the kitchen to watch her as she heads straight back to the fruit cellar and down the stairs, and we hear the door bang.

She was down there until the guests went home and one of the servants was sent to get her.

As soon as she was gone, Peony went down to the fruit cellar to see how much the girl had eaten while locked up, but nothing had been touched.

Peony told us that the girl could expect to be beaten and sold, which made us behave for the rest of the day.

ಸ

That Creek's not comin' today, is she?

Ben had come to the old landing at his usual time. He had his notebook and pencils. Today he wore an old straw hat almost 'xactly like Jonah used to wear. He looked nothin' like Jonah who was much bigger and not a Choctaw.

"No, she's gone looking for some old maps," he said. "We found some old homesteads up Webb's Creek yesterday."

The Jacksons were good friends of Monsieur. Master Pierre used to play with Artimis, who was about his age.

Ben was scribbling as I talked, but I couldn't see that I was sayin' anything important.

There were three houses along the creek then. The Jacksons, and two houses blongin' to the Dodges.

"Two?" Ben asks.

Again, I don't get it. One. Two. It's not hard. There was Mr. and Mrs. Dodge, and they built a house for their son and his wife on their land. His name was Joseph."

Scribble. Scribble.

There are houses on the river side, too, around Granger's Ferry and down to where the rivers come together.

Yes, the inlet leading up to Northaw is across the river from there. The stream wasn't always deep enough to float a keel boat or even a flatboat which is why the ford was built. It saved goin' all the way to the ferry and they didn't have to pay to cross.

I don't know. It was there as long as I can remember. Used more of the year than the boats. Monsieur didn't have that many wagons, so they went back and forth all summer with the cotton with mules they got from somewhere. It went to the warehouses, then to the steamboats.

I was a bit like Minnie when it came to the steamboats. Hearing Jonah tell his stories since I was little, I couldn't help but think what lay down river – or up, for that matter.

It was Peony, again, who talked sense. She asked how many times I saw Madame or Monsieur go anywhere. Truth was, they didn't. I didn't feel too bad after that.

But they *could*.

Northaw

Did I hear anything about trouble brewin'?

I don't know. No one talks to me about it. Oh, trouble came, all right, but somehow, I missed feelin' it. Other people did, I could see that, but for some reason, all that sufferin' never touched me.

Ben's Notes

It was six o'clock when Lahoma left me. I couldn't wait to tell Dolly what she said. I felt stupid about not thinking of a family building a house on their land for their son and daughter-in-law.

Dolly's comment about Creeks and Choctaws having their ups and downs, once again made me realize how little I knew about what people called "my heritage." What people are now has always been more important to me than what others had been.

This was another point that Mr. Rush had made about Geography: it didn't only look to the past, but also to the future. The past that the historians look to is less than a clod of earth to the geographer.

Still, Dolly had hit on something I should look into, especially if Lahoma and her mother were part Choctaw. Knowing what they believed or how they thought might provide a key, if not that, then at least something that could chip at the surface of what – and how – Lahoma might think.

That was something else that I thought most people got wrong these days: they seemed to think that people a hundred, two hundred, four hundred years ago thought just like we do. Had similar values and so on. One thing that people today think is that people in the past didn't have a sense of humor. I think that has led to serious – and tragic – mistakes in understanding the past.

As for my own past, or "legacy," I have to see if Leah knows anything. Choctaw, and Choctaw-Creek issues seem important to Lahoma. I suppose if I were a slave, who I was would be especially important – but being the landowner's illegitimate child might override that.

Another on the long list of things I never had to think about.

I had a meal at home, then went over to Leah's at about seven.

She was always glad to see me, and the children, too. They were upstairs doing homework or whatever they did. Bob was watching a game on TV, and although I knew he supported neither team, he kept up an enthusiastic commentary.

Leah gave me a beer without asking and started back to the sitting room when I asked if I could talk to her.

She immediately jumped to the conclusion that I wanted to know more about Dolly, and I had to interrupt the narrative of her virtues – not the least of which was if I married her, I'd never have to work again.

"I suspected that," I said. "I've already been out on the boat."

I told her the story of finding the ruins and seeing the alligator.

"A bunch of us from school went into the woods and found some ruins when I was a senior in high school," she said.

"You never told me," I said, teasing.

"Well, little brother, you wouldn't have approved, and our parents certainly wouldn't have!" she laughed. "It was mostly an end of school drinking and make-out party."

I didn't need to know this.

"Where were these ruins?"

"Oh, not far. East of where the marina is now," she said, not particularly interested. "I don't know that they're there anymore."

"Were they industrial? Residential? Commercial?"

She shrugged.

"How would I know?"

It was frustrating but typical.

"You said you've seen me sitting by the old landing," I began. "You've never seen me with anyone there?"

"No," she said. "Have you got another girlfriend? Don't mess things up with Dolly!"

"No, I'm not going to do that," I said, with a laugh. "She's too young – and too odd. I've told Dolly about her anyway.

"That girl – the young, odd one – is part Choctaw. A half or quarter, I think. When she talks, she seems to think I know the Choctaw stories, beliefs and legends, and I don't know – or remember any of them. Do you?"

She shook her head.

"That's the other question – the odd girl, Lahoma, met me with Dolly and warned me that she was a Creek," I said. "Do you know anything about Choctaws and Creeks?

"Lahoma wouldn't even talk to her. Dolly had to ask me the questions to ask her."

Leah shook her head.

"I only knew what they taught us at school – and I remember little of that!" she said. "It just wasn't an issue. A third of the class was White, a third was Black, and a third was a mix of Black, White, and various Indians. We never really differentiated since it was all mixed up."

"It was the same in my class."

"It's the same all over the Black Belt," Leah said. "Bella's studied some of this. Maybe she's got a book."

Leah went to the stairs and called Bella and told her what I was looking for, while I watched the bottom of the seventh with Bob.

Bella came down to the kitchen with her book.

"Hi, Uncle Ben," she said, handing me the book. It was a book about Alabama history. "It hasn't got a lot about Indians, but at the back, there are some legends and stories that are pretty good."

Bella was fourteen but had not yet succumbed to hormones that made her hate her parents and family. Her brother, Stevie, was eleven, and loved sports, cars, and horror and war movies. I missed them when I was away. Like many adults, I found children grounding, piercing any pretensions I might have picked up on my travels.

The big joke on this trip was based on my name. The politically correct brigade had got rid of all ethnic brands, so gone were our familiar childhood faces like Aunt Jemima, the Land o' Lakes Indian princess and, of course, Uncle Ben.

Possibly the stupidest PC name change had been that of the Cleveland Indians to the Guardians. (Mind you, the team had had half a dozen names before it was called the Indians.) The team had been renamed by sports writers – at the request of the team - around the time of World War I. The sports writers remembered Louis Sockalexis, one of the team's early players and a Penobscot Indian and chose the name partly to remember and honor him.

That any of these names was actually honoring people and tribes never seems to have crossed anyone's tiny mind. In New England the street names are all either English place names or Indian names. I suppose they'll have to go, too. Too white, or "cultural misappropriation."

Stevie and Bella took great delight in teasing me, understanding the stupidity, saying, "Uncle Ben isn't an Indian!" and laughing loudly when I'd reply, "Oh, yes, he is!"

The truth was, they don't identify as Indians any more than I do.

Leah knew no more than I did. We recalled a few stories we were told as young children, but none was of Choctaw origin. Leah simply repeated what I have already noted: "We're Americans from Alabama."

I watched the rest of the game with Bob and had another beer before going home with the book.

Northaw

12 Ben didn't have the Creek with him today, either, but kept expecting her to show up. I don't know what he sees in her. I'm not havin' her questions.

As if expectin' that woman to show up weren't bad enough, Ben started askin' about Jody, and he didn't get why I couldn't explain. Jody's Jody. Always been with me at Northaw. None of his business.

I like Ben. He listens and doesn't care about me bein' a slave or anything. He doesn't think I talk crazy like other people around do. The Creek thinks I talk crazy though she never says so. Sits there pretendin' to look interested.

Ben wants to know things about what Monsieur and others are callin' "the comin' trouble." I hear 'em talkin', but I don't know what it means. What I can tell Ben about are things like Peony's cookin', the types of apples that was grown at Northaw, the plums, and how, when they're makin' scuppernong wine, everyone gets silly.

But it *is* good.

Buck Market tells about how some plantations make corn whiskey that makes people do strange things and talk too much, but I don't know how they can tell as that's what it seems they do anyways. Monsieur gets wine shipped up from Norleans, but it's kept locked up in a cupboard in the dining room.

Sometimes, the others my age sneak apples and make cider. It doesn't last long and makes us girls giggle and do things we wouldn't without cider; it passes the time.

Yes, it was fun and also some things people don't talk about. I have nothing to hide really. Just the sort of things everyone keeps private to herself.

An' why do you ask about things I want to forget? I don't understand why you want to know about the times I was unhappy, or hungry, cold, sick, sore and scared.

That's not why I talk to you.

About the time I was thirteen, there was typhoid. Slaves were sick and died and so did the whites. One of the managers, Mr. Moran – Buster, they called him – a decent man, lost his wife and son. It broke him and one day no one could find him. Maybe he went into the swamp. Maybe he got a steamboat south.

There weren't doctors around, not like during the war, when there were lots of doctors and hospitals, so we was left on our own to be sick an' to die.

Peony knew such remedies as there were and Monsieur made sure that everyone got some. 'Course some were better than others. The slaves got apple cider vinegar. There was plenty of that. The older slaves got buttermilk, a lot of us ate basil leaves, but the Lefevers took ginger tea and lemon water.

Peony had a secret one which she gave me and Mam and took herself. She'd mix honey and cinnamon into our

Northaw

grits twice a day. Sometimes with cups of water at other times.

Maybe we was lucky, maybe it worked. We lost nine slaves of the thirty, the manager's wife and son, and a man who used to come to us a few times a week to help with shipments and deliveries.

Mam and I would go to bed scared that we wouldn't wake up – or worse, that one of us would and the other wouldn't.

Madame was frantic that Pierre François would die. He did get sick, but not as bad as she made out. Peony saved him, too. I was there to help her, and although he said nothing to me, he met my eyes a few times. I couldn't tell what it meant, it weren't anger or hate. I know those well.

I did feel sorry for him. He looked bad but Peony said his breathin' and pulse were strong. Normally, a slave wouldn't dare touch any in the master's family or any of the whites, but everyone trusted Peony and had respect for her knowledge. With no real doctor for days, what were they goin' to do?

Pierre François made no fuss, and when he improved, even I thought it wouldn't be a good idea to be around in his room. I was glad for him.

Seein' the boatmen put carts with bodies onto the flatboat and pole it over to the graveyards for burial was pitiful. The boatmen were sad and scared and there was talk about ferryin' dead men across the river of death.

These slaves were carefully watched when they handed the white bodies over and when they took the slaves for burial. They didn't want nobody escapin' by pretendin' to be dead.

Jody said that the slaves had to be stopped from pickin' up dirt from the cemetery an' bringin' it back in small bags or pouches because it could help them to escape.

There were a lot of escapes 'bout this time. Some Northern troublemakers had been down getting people excited, and a lot of slaves escaped. Mr. Whitfield lost about twenty over a few years. They was supposed to have put graveyard dirt on their feet. I don't know if it made them invisible or just made them run fast. I don't even know if they *did* escape. It's just what the men said.

The cemetery dirt was supposed to have come from the trips to bury the dead. I asked Rufus why they just didn't bury 'em here at Northaw where they lived, but he said, then there would be lots of cemetery dirt nice and close and, one mornin', we'd all be gone.

He laughed when he said it, but I didn't see the joke.

The sickness lasted for several weeks. Those that were sick but didn't die couldn't work, or if they did, very little. Mam and I, and Peony were all fine. Of the family, only Pierre François got the fever. He was up in about two weeks, but not the same for nearly a year.

He got very thin and couldn't bother to be bossy or argue with Madame.

Northaw

Ben's Notes

"You've got to follow her," Dolly said, firmly. "You're beginning to entertain this notion that she's some sort of visitor from 1850 and not just a deinstitutionalized, delusional and disturbed girl."

I couldn't answer her.

"There's not one thing she's said that couldn't be found online or in the library," she continued. "Look, Ben. History and exploring the area and this period are things I love. And, yes, finding that ruin with you was great. Exciting. But I have better and more fruitful projects than talking to someone who is this far removed from reality."

She was right. This was becoming an obsession. In the past, when confronted with things like this, I'd move on, find a new town, and something else to explore.

I said this to Dolly.

If she cared whether I stayed or left, she didn't show it, and that made me realize that my days in Demopolis were numbered.

"Don't get arrested for stalking but, before investing too much more time in phony recollections gleaned from cheap romance novels, you'd better find out who she is," she said.

We met at the diner and talked about going to where General Lefebvre's house was reckoned to have been, but we both knew there was nothing there to see.

I knew that Dolly was serious about not wasting time, but she wasn't as resistant as it sounds when written down. In the diner over tacos she had joked, "I appreciate the breakfasts and lunches, but if you continue to want my help, you're going to have to take me to a few nicer restaurants, too."

I wish girls would say what they meant. When I told Leah, she said that it was a sign that Dolly really liked me. I said, I thought she just wanted a good free meal.

Dolly and I walked easily along Washington before turning up Commissioners Avenue towards the old ferry landing. We walked slowly. Our hands brushed. We pretended not to notice, but didn't move to avoid them brushing again.

"Who's this Buck Market?" she asked.

"One of the younger slaves, I think," I said. "Lahoma said he was mostly Indian but part Negro.

Northaw

She said he was a good boatman and knew the river, but I don't think he was ever on steamboats."

Dolly considered this.

"Curious name," she mused. "Maybe where he worked before Lefebvre bought him?"

"Possibly. I was thinking it was 'Marquette' which would have the French connection."

Dolly looked at me.

"Not bad, Choctaw," she said with a big smile. "Another name to try to trace."

We walked on in silence.

"Do you think she'll show up today with you around?" I asked.

"She's probably following us now," Dolly replied, but didn't look around. "How many times have you seen her?"

"I don't know. About a dozen."

"And she always shows up?" she asked, then added, "If you say, who could resist you, I'll push you in the river!"

"She seems to."

Dolly thought.

"Well, either she's real, or a projection of your imagination and you've hypnotized me – or drugged my taco – or – "

"Or what?"

Dolly was silent.

"I wish I knew."

We walked to the spot where I always sat. There were some people around enjoying the day, and a group of children watching the boats coming down from the marina.

"Hard to image this was too shallow to sail on," I said, "but it was, most of the year."

Dolly sat down and pulled her knees up and held them as she stared into the Sumter County woods.

"So, are you going to follow her?"

I didn't reply for a moment.

"You know you have to," she prompted.

"I think it would work better if you followed her," I said.

"No way!" she exclaimed.

"Wait. Think about it. Lahoma might expect me to follow her," I argued. "If you leave early then watch her, she can watch me stroll off into the sunset and you can follow her."

When she didn't reply instantly, I continued.

"If she's part Choctaw, she'll know how I'd follow her. Now, a Creek. . ."

Northaw

She bent her forehead to her knees and let out a sound of frustration.

"Oh, all right," she conceded. "It makes some bizarre sense."

"Call me when you get home – or just come by on your way back."

We watched as a barge was nudged up the river. It seemed to move silently, but I expected we'd hear it as it turned away from us. Dolly and I were lost in our own thoughts watching this when we heard a voice.

"Some of those tow boats are longer than the old steamboats," said Lahoma. She was now sitting next to me. "It still takes them days to get to Warsaw, Vienna, Columbus and Aberdeen."

"They are very powerful, too," I said, obviously.

She said nothing but nodded.

"The other day when you were talking about the typhoid – "

She looked sad, then glanced around me to Dolly, then gave a slight frown.

"That was hard to talk about," she said.

"I was just going to ask what time of year it was. You said they used the flatboat, so the water must have been high."

"Late March, I think. The water had already begun to drain away, but the flatboat was fine," she said. "I think there was only one more steamboat each way, but it didn't get above Eutaw."

"Where were people buried?"

Lahoma went quiet and looked around me again at Dolly.

"Does the Creek have to be here?"

"She's helping me – "

"It's all right. I'll go," Dolly said, standing up. "I'll call you later. Goodbye, Lahoma. I really don't wish you any harm."

Lahoma watched her as she left the park and headed down the road to town.

"Monsieur had a foreign religion, so everyone from Northaw was buried in the Old French Cemetery. Whites and slaves," she said. "It were funny, as the slaves kicked up more of a fuss than the whites – and they kicked up a good one. Every time someone died."

She laughed to herself.

"Monsieur didn't say anything about religion, but told people who thought he shouldn't do it that he owned more than an acre of the cemetery and as far as he was concerned, that was part of Northaw, so everyone would be in familiar ground."

She said this with full knowledge of the irony.

"It made us smile when we didn't think we could."

We didn't say much more. We watched the river and talked about the birds diving for fish, or how someone was driving a boat too fast, or how Northaw's fields had been ruined by the building of the locks.

While it was interesting conversation, and Lahoma was undemanding company, I was more aware than ever that she told me nothing that someone who had spent some time in the library couldn't.

Eventually, she stood and simply said, "Goodbye," and walked back in the direction of town.

I watched her until she was out of sight and hoped that Dolly was able to pick her up and not be seen.

It took me about twenty minutes to walk home. I hoped Dolly would call and we could arrange to go to eat somewhere together, but she didn't call until I was halfway through my frozen dinner.

"Did you get lost?" I asked.

She sounded cross.

"No," she said. "Look, I'm sorry I didn't call earlier but I had to do some shopping."

"Did you follow her? Did you see where she went?"

There was silence on the line. I was about to say something when Dolly spoke.

"I followed her down Commissioners Avenue. I was a block behind her and trying to keep in what shadows there were. I was lucky not to get arrested for my odd behavior."

"Where did she go?" I asked, impatiently.

"She crossed the tracks on West Franklin, but before I got there one of the only trains to run this month rolled along, headed down to the paper mill. When it finally passed, she was gone."

Northaw

13 Talkin' about some things makes me remember other things that I don't want to remember, like Mr. Hensley. Ben looks at me. Called himself George, after George Washington.

It's a good thing you didn't bring that girl with you today because she wouldn't like this story.

Around the time of the typhoid when Pierre François was so sick and Madame worried to death, Monsieur wasn't able to keep his eye on things in his usual way. This Mr. Hensley was a Lower Creek. Full blood. He'd been workin' in Wellborn down in Coffee County, and tryin' to do something.

It were after the Creek War. Although the Creeks were beaten by General Scott, he hung around Wellborn and worked as some sort of dealer. He was a freeman somehows, and used to do what he did between Wellborn, Enterprise and Elba and Mobile.

'Parently, Wellborn wasn't much of a place and when the courthouse burned, the county seat moved. Since there were no records anymore, it didn't matter where they put the county seat.

There were some at Northaw who said that the records of Mr. Hensley being a slave went up in smoke and no one could prove it one way or other.

Someone from Northaw met him in Mobile – probly in a tavern – and offered him a job.

Everyone knew it was a mistake to bring him. We were slaves, and they were masters, but things worked along without too much trouble. If there were, it were of the usual sort – drinkin', fightin', takin' the women into the orchard, stealing food, and keepin' the fish we caught.

All those things were true of slaves and whites, and it were the way things were.

But Mr. Hensley was mean.

As a full-blooded Creek, he hated the whites that had driven them from Alabama. He hated the Negro slaves as much as some white men, and he hated Mam, Peony and me.

We were part-Choctaw, a tribe he thought was inferior. Then, we were half-breeds – unlike him – and next, we was slaves.

That meant he could treat us anyway he wanted, and without Monsieur supervisin' as close, he usually did.

Peony cooked for the family and the household slaves. Mr. Hensley treated Peony as his personal cook. If the other managers knew, they didn't say nothin' – or if they did, we never heard about it.

He liked hittin' people, too. It were only when Peony went up the dining room to see Madame about the week's menus, that Madame saw her black eye and bruised arm. Well, it weren't black but purple.

That was probly the only time I saw Madame take any action that didn't affect her or Pierre François.

Northaw

She actually embraced Peony and tol' her not to worry. Of course, knowing how things usually work out, Peony was more scared than ever. It were the first thing other than Pierre François that Madame thought about and her blood was up.

We'd all kept quiet about Mr. Hensley's stealing, his meanness to field slaves, and his messin' with the women an' girls. They all got his attention, 'cept Mam. He's been warned off her by someone, but I was fair game, and had to watch myself in a way I never did before. I was about fifteen.

The way Mam told me was that Monsieur spent time with each of the managers alone, separately, to find out what was happening. Monsieur was clever, too. He also had a private meeting with Mr. Hensley abut somethin' else in the middle of all the other meetin's so he wouldn't be suspicious.

The private chat with Monsieur made him feel more important, and that might have sealed his fate.

Mam said that good managers were hard to find, and Mr. Hensley was needed since Mr. Moran left. This only made some sense because Mr. Hensley was pig-ignorant of boats and the river. Comin' from Wellborn, he'd only seen a river when he went to Mobile. I think he was mean to cover up bein' stupid.

Peony, my friends and I took to carryin' carving knives.

It was funny to see how slaves who didn't particularly like their bosses realized that none of them respected or liked Mr. Hensley.

Mam told me to be especial careful and tell my friends to be, too. She said that Monsieur had a pretty good picture and was figuring the best way of dealin' with it, when one morning a few days later, he'd gone.

Mr. Hensley. Gone.

The river was high and too cold to swim in – not that anyone did – and with the river high, Northaw was on an island. In the spring when it warmed up, it meant the gators were around, and sometimes cottonmouths.

Monsieur organized a search of the whole island, including takin' boats up Doom Creek an' into the swamp. That were funny as no slaves would go and the whites had to do it. They threatened everything but no way would they do it. Monsieur just told the managers to do it before there were a rebellion.

That was another thing on Monsieur's mind.

It took two days to search everywhere – all the stores, cellars, attics and lofts, fruit cellar, wine cellar and the curing barn, baling barn. No sign of him. All his things were still with his bunk.

There was no one to report to, but Monsieur got the word passed up and down the river to the plantation owners. If Mr. Hensley had simply runaway, Monsieur wanted it known that his wages were waitin' on him at Northaw.

I guess that's why I don't like Creeks. She might be nice to you, but I don't want to start carryin' a carving knife again.

No one at the plantation expected him to show up. About a year later, Jody told me why. According to Jody, Mr. Hensley had got way too friendly with Rufus' great-niece, Loola.

More than once, it seems, and Jody said Rufus had taken Mr. Hensley on a walk to see the alligators.

No, it's not funny, Ben, I'm only laughing because it was Loola. The thing is, she wouldn't have minded, but she did like to be asked.

Northaw

Ben's Notes

Against all better judgement, I was becoming very fond of Dolly, but as I could see no future in it, I tried to mirror her professional demeanor and keep my distance. I could tell that's how she saw herself: a professional historian, slowing making her way in the Alabama local history world. It was clear that she loved it. She was focused, methodical, and her intensity could be a little scary.

The day after trying to follow Lahoma, we went to the Demopolis library after meeting for coffee. I had made a list of names and clues which I gave her. I'd been going to the diner enough now that I was greeted as "Mr. Ben" and wherever we went, people said hello to "Miss Dolly," except for a few who insisted on calling her, "Miss Cordelia."

If your small town was friendly, it could feel pretty good living there.

Dolly read my list.

"Evidence of typhoid? George Hensley. Wellborn. Creeks," she said. "I suppose I can understand why she's suspicious of me, but I'm not full-blooded, and neither is she. You'd think that would be some common ground."

We thought as we finished our coffee.

"Right," Dolly said, obviously taking charge. "I'll see if I can find the typhoid epidemic and George Hensley, you see if you can find something about Wellborn. We might get a clue there."

"Where's the Old French Cemetery?" I asked. "I've heard of it, of course, but I'm not sure I ever knew where it was."

Dolly smiled at me.

"You like hard questions, don't you?" she teased. "Everyone is sure they know where it was, but few of them agree. Some say it was what is now Memorial Cemetery. Others that it is towards Arcola, maybe near the Jerusalem Cemetery. Others think other places. Many will say it's underwater, confusing it with the Confederate Cemetery."

They entered the library where everyone greeted "Miss Dolly." She showed me where the maps and references were now, and she looked for the lists of names. Many had taken the names of early owners, which may have been the case with Buck Market/Marquette.

"Give me two hours and I'll buy you lunch," she said.

Two hours in a library wasn't my idea of fun, but I knew it had to be done.

One of the problems was that most of the people we spoke about were slaves and they weren't recorded by name.

In the event, Wellborn was equally elusive.

I turned up a large house known as Wellborn whose owner had been killed in the Creek War in 1841. Finally, I thought, something I can pin down. That was until I read that Wellborn, the house, was on the Georgia border and nowhere near Coffee County.

Twenty minutes later, I had learned a few things about Wellborn, the town. For a brief period, it had been the county seat until a fire in 1851 destroyed the town hall and all the records, just as Lahoma had said. The county seat moved to Elba, and Wellborn disappeared – or became Damascus – which wasn't much help since that's not there anymore, either. Oh, there's a fire station and a senior citizens center that uses the name, but there's nothing else.

Dead end.

I looked at some maps and saw where the old Lock 4 was, and then discovered an aerial photograph that showed it. Better still, it showed Daub's Swamp as dry land as well as where Dolly and I had explored the ruins. Not even a creek showed on the photo.

Was this proof of anything?

I looked across the library and saw Dolly expertly consulting volumes and making notes. I wondered how I was going to fill an hour and fifteen minutes, and looked through my notes to see if there was something productive I could do. Most items were crossed off, having led nowhere. Then, I saw the note about the books that were listed in the back of Bella's school history book and decided to try to find them.

I didn't find the ones listed, but did locate a slim volume of Choctaw lore. I read about good and evil spirits, their creation story; about two brothers who separated, and each took half the people, one becoming the Chickasaw tribe.

It was amazing that none of this had come down to me, but then, I'd talked to people whose families had come from Italy or Greece and they knew not a single word of their legacy language, and their cultural knowledge didn't go beyond food and what the general public knew about Rome or Athens, or spaghetti and moussaka.

That didn't make what I was reading any less interesting, just remote.

The article ran through the usual mythic stories found around the world: a creation story, some disaster stories, brothers falling out, brothers doing great things, great romances, jealousies, betrayals, sacrifices, periods of exile, subjection and redemption.

The differences came in the folk stories and legends rather than in the great myths. Often, these involved animals, men (and women) who were birds, deer, bears – whatever was common in the area – who took shape as humans, or vice versa. These, too, followed familiar patterns.

It was when these stories became linked to places that their local impact and power became greatest.

The spirits around the thousand year old mounds near Forkland – visible from Twelve Mile Bend, the piano playing at Gaineswood, the sightings of ghost steamboats, noises on the stairs and creaks in the attic are what fire the imagination.

For some, like me, those stories are enough. Yes, it's nice to solve mysteries, but once it's solved, it's no longer a mystery.

I looked over at Dolly again. So serious, focused. It made me feel guilty about my daydreaming.

Returning to the text, I began noting some of the Choctaw legends. While I hadn't heard of any of them, something was ringing a bell in my brain or rattling the DNA.

I wasn't sure which.

Searching for more information, I found a list of Choctaw names. I found Leah's and mine (Biisan – which means deer) which I knew. I also knew that Nitaokpulo meant "bear bad." As a child, I thought Chief Badbear sounded badass. I didn't get much of a chance to try it out, though, since my father used the name Bergstrom.

More to the point, I found confirmation that "Lahoma" meant "the people" as she'd told me. Unfortunately, it didn't say what the context was. Was it like the very general, "Inuit" which also meant, "the people" but covered a broad ethnic base? ("Eskimo" at least had the more descriptive meaning, "eats raw flesh.")

Northaw

I consulted an admittedly small Choctaw dictionary looking for Northaw. It had a vaguely Choctaw sound about it like Eutaw and half a dozen other places, but why should a Frenchman call his home Northaw and not Compiègne, Malmaison or Saint Cloud?

I found another book with lists of Choctaw names and found another meaning for Lahoma: beautiful water.

Now, that made some sense.

Northaw

14

I tell you why I don't like Creeks, and you bring her along again? I don't want her to talk to me, an' keep her on your side. *Don't* try to explain yourself, Creek. I know he told you 'bout Mr. Hensley, so's you should know why I feel like I do.

An' I can talk like this because I ain't a slave no more. Only Peony could get away with talkin' her mind at Northaw. I don't know why. Talk was that she was half sister to Monsieur. That made her my aunt or something.

I don't see what you're both laughin' at. Not me, I hope.

Some time after Mr. Hensley was fed to the gator, things got bad. Those that knew about Rufus and the trip to the upper inlet, thought it was because of that. They said it were serious rootwork; that someone knew and had spread some dirt.

I worried for Rufus. He was a good man. I'd known him all my life. He never touched me but to help me – up trees, carry me over the river, and such – but he never resented my place in the household, or that I got treated special sometimes.

As time went on, we began to understand. Jody and me, and Buck would listen to conversations at night, hidin' where no one could see us, just like we did when the house was bein' built. Course, now it were harder because we were bigger an' all.

Some of what we heard almost made us cry out or make noises that would give us away. Other things, I didn't understand no matter how hard I listened.

It was about raising money for a war, buying and making guns, cannon balls and getting' horses. It seemed that more and more slaves were escapin' and headin' North. Guards were placed at cemeteries to keep slaves from stealin' dirt to make them invisible so's they could escape.

There was noises in the woods and the swamps. Strange men coming and going for secret meetings. Locked boxes with metal straps being delivered and collected.

There was talk of buying, spinning and weaving wool, or buying material and bringin' it up from Mexico or Cuba. It seemed that everything got busier. Parties always had the men having serious meetings. It were usual for the men to go off for cigars, card playin' and men's stories, but now there was very little laughter and the men looked worried – all the time.

Mam kept sayin' not to worry, which made me worry more.

Jody was scared, too. Jody was never scared of anythin' but was really frit now.

One day when we went over to town and the steamboat came in, there were cannons on the decks. So many that there weren't much room for supplies. The river was getting low and they didn't know if they'd get much further upstream. The cannon were so heavy the water washed high on the guards.

No, I don't know what the steamboat was called. It were a side-wheeler. It were as low in the water as any boat I seen, and there weren't much water. That was the first year I've seen cotton being sent up stream, too.

Tell the girl to leave now.

No, I got no secrets, but watchin' time flow is better with two.

"Time and the river." That's good, Ben. It's easier to talk to you without the Creek.

I *know* I'm part Choctaw, Ben. It's me. Part white, part Choctaw, probably part Negro, part slave and part free. I know all I need to know by *being* those things, I don't have to know *about* them.

People that knows *about* things don't know the *things* as well as those who *knows the things*.

Examples? For a smart boy you ain't too clever are you? (I wouldn't have said that in front of the Creek.)

What I mean is that if you know a gator, you know what it does, how it eats, when it's gonna move, where it might be. If you knows *about* gators, your mind's gonna be so full of that dumb stuff that you'll be thinkin' about that instead of *knowing where that gator is*, or when he's gonna charge.

Oh, you make me laugh, Ben!

Mr. Hensley knew nothing about nothin'. He certainly didn't know gators, but even if he did, it wouldn't have done him any good.

Why? 'Cause he was a'ready dead when Rufus fed him to them.

That didn't happen much at Northaw. It were a more peaceful place than many.

At other places, it was different. What were called runaway slaves were mostly just chased off the bluffs, or into the swamps, and didn't actually 'scape. That particularly happened when cotton prices were low and the price of slaves.

I couldn't have said all that with the Creek here. I want to talk about nicer things with you, Ben. Things that you 'preciate.

Like the parties. They were pretty and the music was beautiful, and I'd get to meet people from other plantations.

I'd be workin' upstairs for the ones at Northaw, and Madame, although she didn't like "her husband's bastard daughter" – which she always said kindly – I was well behaved, did what I was supposed to – often before I was told – and kept my mouth shut. Madame had a 'ticular dislike of slaves who breathed through their mouths. She said they looked deemented, or plum stupid.

We went to Bluff Hall and Gainesville and Rosemount. There was one we went to by steamboat, but I don't remember where it was. Actually, I don't remember that party, either.

Anyways, sometimes we'd be given good food – Monsieur always served good food to the visiting slaves and maids – but, unless I was working, the time they were dining was the time we could sneak out and meet the new boys.

Oh, don't look like that, Ben. The same thing were goin' on upstairs. Worse, even. Young white girls were being traded for slaves, land or money to marry.

Oh, it could be an upside down world. If a white girl got pregnant, it were a huge scandal. If a Negro girl did, the owner was delighted he'd get another slave for nothin'.

Ben's Notes

When I related the parts of the conversation that she had missed to Dolly, she was red with frustration. So much so that it took her some time to decide what to rant about first. What she said first surprised me.

"You've got to touch her, Ben."

I stared in comprehendingly at her.

"*What*? Why? You think she's a figment of our imaginations?"

Dolly shook her head.

"No figment of my imagination would be so rude to me," she said. "You've seen her a dozen times and haven't brushed hands with her. You haven't seen her eat or drink. Have you seen her perspire? You don't even know where she lives."

"Dolly – "

"She looks like a waif, but isn't grubby. She doesn't carry a purse or bag. No makeup or jewelry."

Although she had stopped, I knew she wasn't finished.

"I had time to do a little research today," she continued. "I was trying to see if there was anything about George Hensley. Nothing. But I looked up Creek names and one that was used to designate that someone was light skinned was Hensley. Lahoma seemed to sense this, if she didn't *know* it, and suggested it was why he hadn't been enslaved."

Coincidence? Calculated? I pondered this, but Dolly wanted to hear a reaction.

"Good bit of research, Dolly," I said, trying to get her to calm down to normal. "How widely known would that be?"

"I didn't know it, but that doesn't mean anything."

We'd driven to one of the better restaurants on Route 80 and sat in a booth not close to anyone else.

"Can we ask Lahoma to come with us for a coffee or something?" Dolly asked. "You may have to do it alone. She'd never come with me."

"I can try," I said, only half paying attention.

Dolly sensed this.

"Why? What are you thinking?"

"Two things. Unrelated," I said. "I was wondering if I went to the river at a different time if she'd show up. I've always gone at about the same time – between four and five – but what if I went at seven in the morning? Do you think she'd come?"

Northaw

Dolly thought for a moment.

"Easy enough to find out. I could be there in the background and maybe see which direction she comes from."

"Shall we do that?" I asked, and Dolly nodded. "Tomorrow?"

"Fine. What was the second thing?"

I smiled.

"Completely different: I was counting up the dead bodies at Northaw," I said, checking my notebook. "Not all were there, but they were known there. Mr. Skitters, Wilson, Hensley, Buxton, Moran – and who knows how many others?"

I was surprised how quickly Dolly rose to their defense.

"That's a period of twenty years in an isolated community on the edge of civilization with – how many? Fifty? Sixty people living and working together?"

She paused remembering something else I'd told her.

"The idea of *saying* that discontented slaves ran away when they were otherwise disposed of was really disturbing, though."

I agreed. As bad as slavery was, murder is another level.

We continued our meal speaking only occasionally until we finished and were having our coffee.

"I'm still looking for one verifiable fact that I can grab hold of," Dolly said. "This is all lovely – if inferior – Margaret Mitchell stuff, but can you get me one simple fact that proves all this time isn't being wasted on the rantings of a dimwitted girl?!"

I had no answer for Dolly, and I very much wanted one. She'd given of her time and emotional energy but, as yet, had nothing to show for it.

"Here's another slight thread you might look at," I said. "Today, Lahoma was talking about seeing war preparations. She never puts dates to anything, and today she couldn't tell me the name of a steamboat claiming she couldn't read – but couldn't she have been told? Or did such things just not matter to her?

"Of course, that presupposes that she is rational. We've no real proof of that, either," I said.

"What's your thread?"

I laughed.

"I appear to have lost it. Sorry. In talking about preparations for war, she mentioned cotton being

Northaw

shipped north on the river," I began, thinking out loud. "Why would cotton be needed upriver?"

We couldn't answer this.

"The cannon being shipped upstream might make some sense. They might want to get supplies near a railroad. Another thing to research," I said, making a note. "But the cotton?"

"Uniforms?"

"Maybe parts of uniforms, but they were wool. Warmer, tougher."

We sat in a comfortable silence. It was the first time it didn't feel awkward. Even the long stretches on the boat had been slightly awkward. There was the scenery and our quest to occupy our conversation but not this comfortable silence.

Of course, once we recognized it, it became awkward, and we both laughed uneasily.

Dolly was the one to break it.

"If you go to the landing at seven tomorrow morning, I'll be there in the background somewhere watching to see where she comes from, if she comes," she said. "I'll stay out of the way, but remember, you must try to make some physical contact. Take some doughnuts and offer her one, or at least some Lifesavers or gum."

She went silent again. Then, after a moment, shook herself and stood up.

We had paid the bill three cups of coffee ago, so she moved quickly out the door. I followed her into the parking lot where she turned around quickly to face me.

"Why are we behaving as though we believe this woman?" she demanded. "She's obviously some sort of nutcase, and we're playing along with her delusions."

It was the same old ground that we were going over again. Dolly seemed to want a different sort of explanation than I did, but I didn't know what it was. I hoped she might find it, but it was time to let her know she'd be on her own.

"Dolly, I'm not going to do the Lahoma thing much longer," I said. "I'm planning to go on the road again. I've had a great visit back to my old hometown. It's been good to see my sister and Bob and the children. They're my only family.

"But, it's time to move on. The beginning of next week will find me somewhere else," I said. "That will give me time for a few more visits with Lahoma, some time for research and time to check all my traveling gear and get the car serviced.

"I've written my piece on Demopolis and it's in line for publication."

Dolly had listened with no visible reaction.

"We must make the most of our time, then," she said.

Northaw

15

I love it here in the morning, Ben. Don't you? The mist rising from the river, so thick that you can't see round the bends. Anything could be comin'. Good things. Bad things. And we won't know until they get here.

Funny this town never grew bigger. Monsieur an' some of his friends had high hopes for it. They talked of schools and hospitals and even the new railroad like the one from Mobile to Meridian. Mr. Lyon said one day it could carry more cotton than a steamboat. Jody and I giggled about that because there's one railroad and lots of steamboats.

So, why you here this time of day? Did you come to see me?

You're right, Ben. I knew you were coming. Don't ask me how. And you're right about me wanting t' tell you my story. No, I can't answer why I want to – need to – tell you my story. I can't even tell you what it is that I want you to know.

You always ask for things in order of time, but when one day is like another for so long, thoughts arrange themselves diff'rent.

You know most of it now. I've not held back any secrets. I might not have remembered everything. I might not have remembered everything right. Only things I haven't told you are the things that I've forgotten myself – oh, just little things like sittin' for hours sewin' Madame's things in the corner of the kitchen while Mam and Peony were cookin' or polishing the copper or silver. They kept everything sparkling while I sat there with a needle, thread and Madame's stockings, or a ripped shirt, or one of her precious gloves. I weren't bad at mendin', but hated ironing. Linen was the hardest. Wool and cotton were forgiving, but not linen.

But you don't care about laundry. Yes, buckets and wash boards and something on a long wooden pole with wooden fingers to wash really well. I'd forgotten the buckets of water that had to be brought in and all the pumpin' we had to do, an' we had to keep a fire goin' even in summer. There was a good well though. It never ran dry, not even that year with the river dried up and the boats got stuck.

Yes, I know I told you about the river before, but not about the well.

What? Did I ever get married? I was old enough to. A lot of the slave girls got married when they was about fifteen. There were travelin' free black preachers who would wander around stopping at steamboat landin's mostly. They'd come off and while the papers were being done, would do some preaching, or a 'tism, or even a weddin'. 'Tisms were funny because no one liked getting all wet, and lots of people – even big men – were scared white for fear of drownin'!

Northaw

Even white folk waitin' for things to happen on the boat would stand at the back laughin' and sometimes clappin'.

There were never many people though. Fifty maybe.

Well, it was because I was Monsieur's that he didn't marry me off at fourteen or fifteen. I already told you that that didn't stop me from havin' some fun, but I was particular and people knew to stay away from me – unless I encouraged them, of course.

I think Monsieur had some plans in mind but they changed when Master Pierre François got engaged, but I'll come to that.

Did I dream of bein' free? 'Course. It's kinda funny because so many of the people I saw who were free weren't very happy. They was complainin' and bickerin' always fightin' about somethin'.

But, who doesn't want to be free?

My trouble was that I didn't 'xactly know what it meant. I had no money. I couldn't do anything no one else could. I had nowhere to go – and didn't know what was beyond Demopolis anyway.

And then there was the cruelty. 'Part from Mr. Hensley, I didn't see much cruelty. I saw plenty of pain from all sorts of things, but not much cruelty. I knew it existed at other plantations and some said factories were even worse – but I couldn't imagine a factory.

People would get injured in cotton gins and big machines, and the owners and others would complain about the cotton ruined by the blood and how they'd have to hide it in the bale. There was meanness, but I was spared cruelty.

You got me talkin' about that stuff and I didn't even see that it had turned into a beautiful bright morning. You can see all the way up the river now and hear the town comin' to life.

Coffee? Breakfast? That's very kind, Ben. Thank you. Truth is, I don't know you well enough to accept your invitation.

But it's not just coffee is it?

No, it's all right, Ben. You just stay put.

There was more and more talk about freein' slaves from Yankees who were comin' down to make trouble. I heard Monsieur and his friends talk about it. Wanted to upset our whole way of life. That was something they said again and again. And that led to war talk.

Why do you always ask about dates. I never knew what day it was. I knew the wet and dry months and the winter and summer and when the river was high or low, *but what year was it?* What did it matter?

Again with the where do I live? I live at Northaw. You live on West Jackson and the Creek lives in The Cove. I don't know where anyone else lives. Oh, your sister, she lives on West Jefferson with her husband and children.

What else have I got to do all day? Your sister's nice. It's fun to see her with the children, walkin' to school. Maybe that's what I'd have been like if I were free.

Why would I hurt them – as if I could? Have I hurt you or your girl?

Now, don't you be dishonest with me, Ben. She's your woman.

No?

Well, I guess she just ain't told you yet.

Ben's Notes

I hardly knew how to begin to relate any of this to Dolly. There were too many things going on in my head: Lahoma being there at seven in the morning; her talk about being free; keeping boiling water in the kitchen, Pierre François' talk about coming changes, preachers and baptisms next to steamboats, and her comments about only being aware of seasons and not years.

This interested me as it gave an insight into how slaves might have thought. Apart from those involved in planting and harvesting, time was endlessly linear. They probably never saw a clock – and couldn't read it anyway – and simply went where they were led and did as they were told. They might know something of Sundays but there was no guarantee of that.

Of course, they would observe the seasonal changes, see children born and grow, but the idea of a June a year later from this June may never have occurred to them.

Later, when I told her, Dolly observed that this was a clear demonstration of the difference between lack of knowledge and ignorance – the latter being willful, she maintained.

What really had confused my thoughts was Lahoma's final remark about Dolly, "She's your woman."

That at once terrified me and ignited a fuse of possibilities that could lead to - ? Well, to who knew what.

I called Dolly to tell her I was on my way to meet her at the diner. She laughed and said she was already there, drowning in coffee waiting for me to show up for breakfast.

"When I got to an observation place, I could hardly see across the street," she said, once I sat down. "I could hear nothing and see nothing. About ten minutes before you got there, I walked very quietly towards where she usually sat, approaching from an oblique angle.

"By the time I got to a place where I could actually see anything, you were both there."

I heard what she said, but was distracted, still thinking about what Lahoma had said. Had Dolly shown any pleasure in seeing me? Was there anything in her body language to hint at what Lahoma suggested? I'd seen nothing.

I told Dolly what Lahoma had said about the early mornings and her other observations. I also advanced my theory about a different perception of time. She was unimpressed.

"From the very beginning, Lahoma told me that I was obsessed with dates and chronological order, whereas, she said her thoughts were grouped differently," I said.

Dolly brightened.

"Okay, I see how that might have worked," she said. "They may have had a way of ordering thought or memory like the ancient *loci*, as well as the obvious oral tradition."

"Yes, memory palaces," I said, and Dolly nodded.

I thought some more, staring at the bacon on my plate.

"If you strip out chronology, then the oral traditions transform into tales and fables rather than strict historical accounts," I said, puzzling it out as I spoke.

"It's the way people see major religious texts like the *Bible* if you take away the idea that it is *literally* true," Dolly said. "The things in the same niche in the memory palace are all related, but not necessarily chronologically."

I thought about this.

"They can be sorted by color, texture, sound, place – all sorts of criteria other than time," she continued.

"So how does that help us with Lahoma?" I asked. "Does it bring us any nearer to understanding who she is or if she's simply a local loony?"

Dolly sighed, sat back and shook her head.

"Good step in trying to understand her thought process," I said.

Dolly smiled and leaned forward.

"Are we able to deduce at least that she is not a projection of us in that we don't think that way?" she asked.

This was getting too deep for me, but I didn't want Dolly to see that.

"Yes, I think we can," I said, to sound supportive. "But how does that get us any further."

We finished our breakfasts talking about other things: people we knew from Demopolis, her father's political ambitions, how she had to get her blog material up to date.

While finishing her coffee, she looked at her watch.

"The library will be open now," she said. "I want to see if I can find places in town that look after mental health patients."

"And then?" I asked, as we walked.

"Visit them," she said, resolutely. "It would surprise me if any of them let their patients out before seven in the morning, so I'm not expecting much."

She paused with a new thought. She seemed hesitant as she turned to look at me.

"You haven't done the obvious, you know," she said, not quite accusingly.

"I've thought about it," I said, knowing exactly what she was thinking.

"It's a question of risk, and so far, I don't think the risk is worth it."

"But taking a picture of her would be so easy," Dolly protested.

"But what would it prove?" I retorted. "That could piss her off and I'd never see her again, and we'd never get to the bottom of it."

"Perhaps, but you've seen her more than a dozen times, and you're not getting anything new – "

"That's not true," I interrupted. "She's always giving new stuff. It's just not verifiable – yet."

"And probably never will be," Dolly added.

"She sees me writing everything down, and she doesn't object. I get new names every day."

"Well, you get a picture tomorrow."

Once at the library, I resumed reading about the Choctaws, but my thoughts continued to bounce between the wondering how Lahoma would react to a picture, and what she had said about Dolly and me.

Those thoughts were suddenly banished by the words I had just read. I went back to the beginning of the passage. It was more about Choctaw legends. Most of it washed over me as irrelevant to what I thought I was looking for, but these few sentences could hold the key.

I picked up the book to take it to Dolly who was in the main area.

"Please don't take reference books from the reference room," a voice said, shattering the silence and freezing me in the way my old sixth grade teacher's did.

I looked up to see a librarian shaking her head at me.

Contritely, I put the book back on the table with my things and went to fetch Dolly.

She was unhappy about being dragged away from her old maps and ancient directories, but she came to my table and sat as I pushed the passage in front of her.

Among the chief Choctaw beliefs was that of two souls. One was an earthly life force (shilup, or inside shadow) that died with the individual, and the second was an immortal soul (shilombish). The shilombish could travel between the physical world and the world of the dead. It was believed that it visited the deceased's old friends and encouraged them to join him in the spiritual world.

Dolly said nothing when she finished reading, but stared at me.

"Here, look at this bit, too."

I turned a page and pointed to another section.

The Biskinik, or "news bird" was a harbinger of news, usually that would arrive that day. Like the shilombish, it could travel between the world of the living and the world of the dead. It could be the bearer of good news or of warnings. Descriptions suggest an American blue jay.

16

Why of course you can take my picture, Ben. It would be an honor, though I don't know why you'd want to. Madame and Monsieur had their pictures taken not long before Pierre François' wedding. They looked pretty stiff, but thought enough of it to have it in a big brass frame on the mantlepiece in the parlor.

You do like the early morning, don't you, Ben? It's very foggy and there's a thick mist on the river. You able to take a picture without sunlight?

He does ask some odd questions. Today he asked if I thought the camera he was using was strange. How would I know? I've never seen a camera before. Anyway, I stood with my back to the river, and it would have given a good view had you been able to see anything.

The only strange thing about the camera was that the picture was in color and the one of the Lefevers weren't. He asked if I was surprised to see myself, but I wasn't as I'd seen myself plenty of times, in mirrors, reflections in windows, and in the still waters. I told Ben this and said that there were something not right with his picture.

It took a bit of puzzling, but Ben worked it out. He said the reflection were somehow backwards but photographs were the way people saw us. I don't see why they had to make it different. It doesn't change who we are.

He took two pictures. One with me looking at him, and one of me looking up the river, dreamin' like. I might have dreamed if I could have seen anything.

I asked him how Dolly the Creek was. I suppose I'd better not be too rude if he's gonna take up with her. I don't mind upsettin' her, but Ben's carin' and kind.

He asked if I wanted to get something to eat, but I didn't. He asked what I did most of the day when I wasn't talkin' to him. I told him I was at Northaw, of course. I had my work there.

He were full of questions today. He asked if I knew Choctaw legends or stories. I don't know when he thought I had the chance to learn any of that. The only learnin' I did was numbers, and I'm good at them, but as I've told him before, I can't read 'cept for numbers. That were a language I can understand.

Ben told me he was going away next week. Dolly the Creek is gonna to have t' act quickly if she doesn't want him to escape – which she don't.

We sat on the damp grass and looked toward the river. I asked him if he could smell it. He said not really. I can. I told him that what I said earlier about time wasn't right. Not entirely.

I knew the names of most of the months, but would forget the order, but I could tell where we were in the year by the depth and smell of the river.

Northaw

I laugh, which surprises Ben, so I have to explain to him about the great flood after the great drought.

About two years when the winter rains weren't enough to float a flatboat, we had rain almost every day in July. That ruined a lot of crops and the cotton price went high – but no one had enough cotton to get rich on. The river flooded and stirred up mud and silt and washed away trees and floated fallen logs and branches into the river. More steamboats were wrecked that year than anyone could remember. Deadheads they called them. They say they can rip the bottom off a steamboat and sink it faster than anything. (Low hangin' branches – low because the river was high – could knock down stacks, wheelhouses and Texas decks.)

Since there was nothing the slaves could do in the fields, they set about buildin' levees to reclaim some fields – or to prevent it happenin' again.

Fortunately, the next few months were good and a lot of crops could be salvaged. It weren't great, but it were better than the drought year.

Men that visited said that it was all part of the bad luck the South was havin', and that, no doubt, the North was behind it somehows.

Do you know what it's like to hear people talkin' and not have an idea what they're goin' on about? I un'erstand more now, somehow, but I didn't then.

I laugh at Ben again. No, I didn't go to school in between! It comes with age, I guess.

There were more people givin' speeches at the landings about gettin' rid of slaves. Some people said what the Northerners meant was gettin' rid of them by killin' 'em. That scared a lot of us, and mean slave owners kept sayin' it. They said that "setting them free" meant setting them free from this earth.

Monsieur wouldn't have that talk at Northaw. Mam said he had some strange French ideas about equality and brotherhood, but he still had slaves like us. Madame was much more clear about what she believed and never needed to explain it to anyone. It were clear.

Around that time, Northaw lost a few slaves. There hadn't been trouble, but according to Buck Market, a few of them kept talkin' about things and got themselves so scared that they decided to make a run for it. Buck said it was a lot of money that just disappeared mos' likely into the swamp, or drowned in the river.

Mam taught me to look after myself, an' keep away from trouble. She also said, that sometimes trouble just came lookin'.

No, nothin' like that.

Do you ever feel that you've just been too lucky? That your life might have been just too easy?

By the time I was about nineteen, I started thinkin' like that. There were trouble all around – maybe it was the

Northaw

floods, or the droughts, or the things them Northerners was talkin' about, but things began to feel uneasy.

Sure, I were a slave, and I worked hard and long, but I was fed, had a place to sleep, clothes to wear, and occasionally people was nice to me. Mostly they were indifferent, but that was better than bein' yelled at, hit or beaten. I seen the scars on some of the men – even some of the women.

I got an uneasiness with all the talk of comin' trouble and didn't know what it was about. It was like a fear growin' inside. Somedays, I wouldn't feel it or think about, but sometimes it was like when you're hungry an' you couldn't think about anything else.

Ben's Notes

I waited at the door for the library to open. The first order of business was to print eight-by-ten prints of the pictures of Lahoma. I'd take them to the diner where Dolly was going to meet me.

By the time the librarian – the one who had told me off the day before – opened up, turned on the lights and all the equipment, put on the coffee pot and a dozen other things librarians appear to do each morning – I had to struggle to be my normal charming self and not point out that "Open at 9:00" should mean open and ready to do business.

However, the quality of the prints were worth waiting for and the image stood out on the glossy paper. As she slipped them into an envelope (another fifty cents), I asked her to take a look at them and asked if she recognized the girl.

She gave one of those "I have better things to do" looks that they must teach in library science courses but looked anyway.

"Do you know who she is?" I asked. "I expect you know most people in Demopolis."

She shook her head as she looked at Lahoma.

"No, I don't know her," she said, then looked at me suspiciously.

"I met her at the landing. It was too foggy to take pictures of the scenery, so I asked if she'd pose," I improvised. "She walked away as soon as I shot them. I'd give her copies if I knew who she was."

The librarian looked back at them.

"I've seen her about – around the old landing, where this was taken – but don't know who she is or where she lives," she said, her manner softening. "Pretty in an old-fashioned way."

I thanked her and left.

Dolly was enjoying a cup of coffee and turning the pages of a house renovation magazine when I arrived at the diner.

She smiled as I sat down but remained distant. If what Lahoma said was true, I expected Dolly might try to touch me in some little way.

The waitress came and we ordered breakfast. She didn't have to show us menus.

"Here," I said, handing Dolly the envelope. Better look at these before the food arrives."

She carefully withdrew the two prints and looked at them. She stared for several minutes at the one where Lahoma was just facing the camera.

Northaw

"She looks like a normal girl," she said, sounding disappointed. "A bit plain in her dress, but she doesn't look pale, sick, mad, or anything out of the ordinary. The hair's a bit curious, but everyone's is these days. Not a particularly imaginative pose."

Our breakfasts arrived and Dolly put the pictures back in the envelope.

"Did she tell you anything else you didn't know?"

I explained how she had told me about her sensations at the approach of the Civil War, how slaves were running away, even from Northaw.

Dolly was amused when I told her how Lahoma had said she had no idea what a camera looked like even though the Lefevers had had their pictures taken.

"I'd love just one name or place to be able to be verified."

I felt the same way and told her that she'd eventually find one piece and that a bunch would reveal themselves after the first. She was less optimistic.

"While waiting in the library, I was thinking that of all Lahoma has told us, she hasn't once given us anything anachronistic," I said. "Everything has been period perfect."

Dolly thought about this as she ate and nodded.

"She's made no mention of anything modern, either. She hasn't questioned the way we look, motorboats on the river, the telephone polls, the cars – anything."

"It's almost as though she didn't see them," I said. "No, that's not right. She talked about the modern tow boats."

"She must have seen that train the other day," Dolly agreed.

"Or did she walk right through it?"

Dolly was about to give me a sharp reply when she realized I was joking.

"Did you touch her, today?" Dolly asked.

"Briefly. When I held up the phone for her to see the pictures. She steadied it with her hand and our fingers touched."

"And?"

"She didn't feel like a corpse," I said, laughing.

Dolly gave me her exasperated look.

"Warm? Cold? Dry? Clammy?" she prompted. "And scent?"

"Normal," I said. "No Great Sucking Swamp smells, either."

At least this got a laugh from Dolly.

Northaw

The waitress cleared our plates and refilled our coffees.

"Did you know I had a job here, waiting tables?" she asked. "It was during the summer vacation."

"And how did you like that," I asked, laughing as I tried to imagine Dolly juggling plates.

"I loved it," she said, enthusiastically. "It was busy and hard work, and there was a lot to think about, but the people were nice, and I had some fun conversations with the regulars. Caught up with some old friends, too. I might have served you!"

It was a tease, but it marked a change in her manner.

"How long did you do that for?"

Her face changed.

"A week," she said, looking cross. "A friend of my father said he'd seen me here, and Daddy went into his, 'No daughter of mine' speech, and made me quit."

"I can imagine you'd be very good at it in a place like this with regulars," I said. "Not, perhaps, at one of the ones on Route 80."

Dolly laughed.

"That's a different breed."

"What did you do instead, or did you have a pampered, work-free summer?"

Dolly sighed.

"I copied and filed legal documents in my father's office. Everyone called me 'Miss Cordelia,' and I only worked half days. It wasn't 'ladylike' to do more."

Dolly saw me open my mouth.

"No, Ben. You are *not* going to meet my father!"

That wasn't even close to what I was going to say, but I decided to keep my mouth shut.

She pushed her coffee cup aside and made sure the table in front of her was clean and dry. She then picked up the envelope with the photographs and drew out the second one.

"This is something else! Even with the fog," she exclaimed. "Look at that profile. That is a dignified Indian face, set against time and the elements. Her gaze gives you the impression that she is seeing things that we – "

She stopped dead and her face paled.

There was a look of horrified incredulity, and she slid the picture across the table to me.

"Have you looked at this closely?" she asked, in a whisper.

Northaw

I didn't reply. I hadn't. I'd just checked to ensure that Lahoma was in focus.

The picture was flat on the table in front of me, and I studied Lahoma's features closely.

"No, not her," Dolly said. "There!"

She struck the paper with a painted nail, and I looked. It was mostly fog over the river, but then I saw what she had.

Barely emerging from the fog were two broad, black vertical shapes that looked like the stacks of a steamboat.

Northaw

17 There was a curious thing when I was about nineteen. It was very hot and there was about an hour between chores. I'd been mending for Madame. I did some ironing too. The irons were hot and heavy, and we needed to be careful so as not to burn ourselves or what we was pressing, an' soon I'd have to start helpin' Peony with the cooking, and then serve in the dining room.

I went out into the orchard – Peony gave me a basket in case someone asked what I was doin'. I picked some berries on the way down to the stream, but then sat there in the shade of an old tree and watched the Spanish moss drift slowly back and forth.

I must have been dreamin' pretty good, because the footsteps were really close when I heard them. It were Pierre François. I scrambled to get up, but he surprised me and told me to stay put. He came and sat next to me – not close, but proper distant.

"I want to tell you something that I don't want you to hear from anyone else first," he said. "I am to be married."

Well, it was a surprise. I hadn't heard that from anyone, and when I thought about it later, I could see how thoughtful of him it was to tell me. At the time, I wished him well. It weren't for me to ask questions, but I did ask if he'd be living at Northaw.

He shook his head. I thought he looked sad.

"There's a plantation near Coffeeville – that's nearly a hundred miles away by steamboat," he said. "It's called River Bend. Mr. Tucker owns it and I'm marrying his daughter, Miss Belinda."

"That's big news, Master Pierre," I said. "I hope you will be very happy."

It weren't much, but I couldn't say much.

"I've only met her twice," he said. "I didn't like her the first time. She was all stuck up, and it was like dancing with a scarecrow.

"Second time, it was here, so you will have seen her. She was still all stiff and proper, but we were able to talk a little," he said, "and I liked her a bit better."

I looked at him. He didn't look *un*happy, but he didn't look in love neither.

"After they went home, Papa told me I was going to marry her," he said.

I thought his voice sounded dead.

"He told me it was a good family. The plantation was a lot bigger than Northaw, and that Mr. Tucker was elderly and would want me to run it soon," he said. "He has nearly two hundred slaves."

"Is it a nice house?"

Master Pierre thought and gave a slight shrug.

"It's bigger than Northaw, but it rambles all over the place. It was built at all different times and doesn't have the strong pillars that Northaw does."

Northaw

It made me feel good to hear him talk about his home that way. To me, Northaw was what a house should be.

"And Miss Belinda?" I dared to ask. "Will she make you happy?"

He looked at me, and it was like a red flash runnin' across his face. This was a sister question, not a slave-servant question, but he softened and smiled.

"I hope so, Lahoma. I really hope so."

We sat in silence for a while, just watchin' the stream.

"One thing," he began, with a little more confidence, "she's as scared as I am – not that I told her I was scared, but we both know what's happening."

I didn't dare say anything about that, so we went back to sittin' and lookin' at the water. Once or twice a fish broke the surface leaving circles running out in all directions. The stream didn't flow too fast there.

I was lost in thinkin' so when Master Pierre spoke again, it startled me.

"Do you ever go down to the water at night – the big river? There are some logs a ways down from Glover's Ferry that were left on the land and sometimes I go and sit on them and watch the river, and the stars, and sometimes, you can see torches or fires across the river. Mostly, you can see stars. Round about August, you can see shooting stars, and on the nights when there is no moon, you can see stars you can't see any other time, and it makes me wonder.

"What also makes me wonder is when a steamboat comes by. When it makes the turn up towards Tuscaloosa, I try to guess whether it's a side-wheeler or a stern-wheeler before it gets to me.

"I think about where it's going, what it's carrying, and who's on board, and I wonder if I'll ever get to the places it will stop," he said, sounding sad.

Then after a moment, he perked right up.

"You know what's exciting at night, apart from seeing the lights on the steamboat and hearing the water splashing is seeing the sparks fly out of the stacks. At night, you don't notice the smoke as much – though you can smell it – but if she's sparking, that can be a real sight."

Not long after, he stood up and straightened his clothes. He was happy with himself again, and I was glad to see it.

He didn't say goodbye but gave his smile and nodded and left.

I stayed by the stream. I could smell the apple trees. They didn't smell like apples yet, but you knew it were apples on the way.

Master Pierre didn't say when he'd be gettin' married, or when he'd be leaving Northaw, but Coffeeville was about as far as Tuscaloosa, if he were right. We didn't have many visitors from either of those places, so I wondered if I'd ever see Master Pierre again.

Northaw

You think I was silly to be sad about that? He weren't bad. There were enough men to talk common sense to him, and he took it pretty well – even if it were from some of the senior slaves, like Peony, Jonah or Rufus. Mostly, it were the managers who told him to behave and between them and whatever Monsieur said to him, he'd be all right.

I thought about what he said about watchin' the stars and the steamboats headin' up to Tuscaloosa and wished I had the time to do things like that. By night-time, all I wanted to do was sleep. The morning would come early enough, an' I could have dreams in my bed.

Besides, there were snakes, gators and ishkitini about.

Northaw

Ben's Notes

"What's an ishkitini?" Dolly asked, in amazed amusement.

We were sitting in the Public Square enjoying the sunshine which had broken through almost as soon as I left Lahoma and the landing.

By chance, I had come across ishkitini at the time I found shilombish, so it was with mock authority that I replied.

"Oh, it's another Choctaw legend. Ishkitini took the form of an owl and prowled the night to kill animals and humans," I said. "Many a stray corpse or dropped poached animal was attributed to ishkitini."

"Are you making this up?" she asked, with the hint of a smile.

"I told you, Dolly, all this stuff is new to me. I grew up as Ben Bergstrom."

We sat there quietly. I think we both wanted to look at the photograph again and study the smokestacks in the fog but were feeling spooked – again – and were delaying facing it.

"What did you make of that story about Pierre François?" Dolly asked.

I shook my head and sighed.

"I'm completely sucked into this," I said. "I thought it rang true. As usual, there was nothing specific that could verify the story, but the idea of a young chap facing an arranged marriage confiding in his half-sister is very plausible.

"Adding to its plausibility was that in her story, neither of them got sentimental. That seemed very real to me," I continued. "Pierre's concerns were believable, too. On one level, they were simple and basic, but on the other, he had a sense of a bigger picture, as if recognizing himself as a pawn in this."

Dolly stood up.

"If you're really going next week, we don't have much time to make sense of this," she said. "There are only a handful of places looking after people who suffered from mental illness. None of them recognized the picture of Lahoma, or even recognized the name."

Dolly's matter-of-fact manner was becoming more caustic.

"We're not finding anything in the library or online," she said. "I think there's only one thing left to try," she said. "And then we can confront her – once and for all."

"What's that?"

"We've got to find Northaw."

☙

In spite of her abrupt manner, Dolly treated this proposal as an adventure – a road trip on the river, as it were. She went whole hog, too, as they say a lot down here. We drove to Vowell's to pick up food for a picnic – which I suspected Dolly had planned regardless of what my conversation with Lahoma had brought.

Loaded with bread, cheese, smoked ham, yoghurt, twelve liters of bottled water, fresh fruit and a tub of coleslaw, she drove to The Cove where we went straight to the boat.

The *Dolly* was, mysteriously, uncovered and ready to cast off.

I decided it was prudent to refrain from comment.

"Where are you thinking of heading?" I asked, after casting off and climbing aboard.

"There are charts below, but I thought we'd run up to Glover's Ferry and head back slowly," she said. "We might be able to see where the ford was, too."

I watched as she exited the canal and joined the river.

"Take the wheel," she said, and stepped down from her chair and disappeared below.

At our slow speed and no traffic, this was not a challenge but it was unexpected. When she returned with several charts, I moved to hand back to her but she told me to stay put.

She unfolded a chart and placed it before me.

"This is where Glover's Ferry was reckoned to be," she said. "Just over the tip of the bend. I don't think there's any evidence you can see from the water. There might be signs of old roads either side. I've never looked for them."

She opened a taped map pieced together with multiple pages of an old map, and we struggled to keep it from flapping about until she folded it to show the area she wanted to talk about.

"There's where it says Glover's Ferry was, but it's slightly different on other maps, but there's only a few hundred feet in it.

"And look at this," she pointed to a section along the southern end of Daub's Swamp. "Look how much more land was visible. There were inlets all along this section."

It was clear that while large areas had flooded, others appeared to have silted up and the streams found other exits.

She let me continue to drive. We passed the marina and Culpepper's Slough, and made the turn up the Black Warrior towards Tuscaloosa.

While Demopolis wasn't the center of civilization, where we were now could easily have been the most remote point on the earth. Apart from the Spanish moss, I thought this could have been up some tributary of the Amazon where "the man who liked Dickens" lived.

Dolly was checking the charts against what she saw, looking back and forth at both sides of the river. They were all devoid of distinguishing features as far as I could tell.

"Slow down," Dolly said, and I pulled back on the throttle "Over there."

She pointed at a dirt and gravel slope running into the river.

I cut the engine, and we drifted back to the spot and looked closely. We were far enough out so we weren't in danger of bottoming out. I started the engine and kept it ticking over just so we could hold our position.

Dolly disappeared below again and came up with a line.

"You wanted to take soundings, see how deep we are."

She handed me the weighted line as I stepped down from the seat. There were knots every fathom but the final fathom had knots every foot. I dropped it.

"Eight feet."

As I pulled the line in, Dolly accelerated and headed across the river to find the other landing. We cruised and drifted several times along the shore but couldn't see anything that might have been a landing.

"Not surprising," Dolly said, "but disappointing. Let's see if we can find the inlet to Northaw."

We progressed at a snail's pace. There were areas that looked like they might have been inlets but weren't. Then, she cut the engine.

"What do you see there?" she asked.

"A few rocks," I said, unenthusiastically.

She swerved the boat across the river again and we searched the opposite shore and stared into the thick undergrowth.

Dolly pointed.

Northaw

"You could almost convince yourself that there had been a road there."

She cut the engine to idle.

"Drop the anchor."

I did and hauled us back to the position near the ghost road we'd sighted.

"Try taking a sounding."

"Six feet. One fathom."

"Take one from the other side of the boat."

I hauled the line up and dropped it in on the river side.

"Seven feet."

Dolly nodded.

"What was the bottom?"

Then, I understood.

"It was rock – both sides."

"And at the ferry landing?

"Mud."

Northaw

18

After talking to Pierre François, I talked about it to Jody. I was wondering why he would spend all that time to talk to me. Jody said there was two reasons: he was scared, and he had no one else, and I was sort of kin. I laughed an' told Jody that was three reasons. Jody weren't as good at numbers as me.

It weren't long after that things began happening. Plans for the wedding. The Tuckers comin' up from River Bend to see Northaw and talk all sorts of business.

When I saw Mr. Tucker, I recognized him as someone who had been to Northaw before. He looked a lot older than Monsieur, but they got on well enough. This time, he came with his wife and his daughter. I don't think Madame liked Mrs. Tucker much, but as Monsieur later told her, she didn't have to, but I could tell what she thought of her and Miss Belinda.

As for Belinda. Well, whatever the distance between us there was didn't stop me from wanting to tell her that she'd better be good to Pierre François. Jody stopped me, of course, which were lucky as when I saw her I realized that the poor girl had about as much freedom as I did.

Her mother told her when to speak and when to stand up and sit down, and from what I could tell, she and Pierre François hardly had time to talk alone. Neither smiled and they barely looked at each other.

For the next months, parcels of all sorts arrived and had to be collected from the steamships in Demopolis. Presents, cloths, fabric – one day Monsieur declared when more boxes were delivered that Madame had probably received more than the bride and it were a good thing that all Pierre François needed was a suit and a haircut.

Along with this, there was more talk of trouble, cotton prices, rail roads – I didn't know what they were – and dishonest cotton brokers. At least there were no more shootings or alligator feedings.

Why doesn't the Creek come with you any more, Ben? I'm laughing because you don't know what to say. Did I frighten her, or does she really trust you with me?

That's a tough question isn't it, Ben? If she hasn't told you how she feels, then she can't complain about you meeting me without her. Don't act surprised. I might be a slave but I've seen a lot. Ben, it doesn't matter.

You know that for a reason I don't know, I have to tell you my story. It doesn't really matter if you believe it, but I think you and the Creek know that I have to tell it.

Why to you? I don't know. I think it would be better to tell it to someone important. You're not that different from me, but maybe that's the reason.

These are the pictures you took yesterday? The colors are pretty. It's pretty much the way I look in a mirror.

Northaw

Those? Why you know what they are! Don't tease me. I don't know why they didn't blow the whistle. I love that sound.

Sometimes, on rainy nights, I'd hear the rain on the roof and outside on the leaves and terraces, there would be the sounds of frogs but most other animals would be quiet, and the blast from the steamboat would cut through the rain. I'd think about the people on board, having a meal, dancing, listenin' to music and playin' cards and gamblin'.

Watchin' one of those bright, pretty boats go by all lit up was like seeing something that was magical, but somehow good, too.

When the Tuckers came, Mrs. Tucker complained about how long it took and said her bed on the steamboat was uncomfortable. Mr. Tucker later joked to Monsieur that it was her that was uncomfortable and that she had kept him awake all night with knees and elbows.

She also complained about all the lurchin' and back n' forthin' on the tight bends that the steamboat couldn't get around, an' how they'd hit bottom from time to time and things would fall over on the table and spill.

Did that Creek drive her boat any better than that? Yes, I saw it. You was lucky you weren't killed goin' up Doom Creek. No one likes going up there. Snakes slither down the hangin' moss and drop on people on the flatboats and keel boats. Fortunately, they only had to use it when loadin' tobacco, an' I already told you there wasn't that much of it. Only one slave got bit, but that were enough to frighten the rest for 'bout ten years.

Only time that inlet were safe was when it was dry in the middle of summer. Even then, it could be swampy from the springs or big pools that didn't dry up. I didn't have to go there much.

Dates? Oh, Ben, you know better than to ask about dates. Dates don't matter. People do. Life does.

Peony used to say that a good life was one that you got through hurting as few people as possible, and then only as much as they needed to be hurt.

I think she added that to cover makin' children behave. There were only a few times I saw her get really mad – like the time she put the girl in the fruit cellar. 'Part from times like that, her scoldin' was normal.

Mostly, she made people happy with her cookin'.

I tried to make people happy, but my main aim was to keep out of trouble. Peony looked after me because I was like her, and Mam to another extent. Being Choctaw, we wasn't like the other slaves, and being related to Monsieur was both good and bad. Good because we got treated a little special, and bad for the same reason.

Can I see those pictures again, Ben?

I used to have a scar, right there near my chin from when I fell down the brick steps to the house. I thought I was goin' to get into real trouble as I wasn't supposed to use those steps. I got nearly to the top and then Madame came onto the balcony and I tried to run down them before she saw me.

She heard my scream when I fell, an' ran down and picked me up before anyone else got to me. I was so scared. She dragged me back up and into her dressin' room – where I was *never* allowed to go – and scolded me loudly. At the same time, she soaked her kerchief in the water jug and wiped my chin clean as gently as she'd touch a baby. She pressed a clean towel against it and told me to hold it. All the time saying how stupid I was and how dare I use those stairs.

She rinsed the kerchief again, and still carrying on, washed my eyes and dried my tears. She looked at my chin a few times until she was happy that it wasn't still bleedin'.

"Now get out of here and don't even think of doing that again," she shouted, the same time she gently stroked my hair to put it in order.

What did I do? What would *you* do, silly?

I said, "Thank you, Madame,' and ran!"

I told you I never made her out.

I haven't made you out yet, either, Ben.

You ask me why I come here, but you never say why *you* do.

Ben's Notes

We pulled up into the inlet that Dolly had seen. It was close, hot, and looked exactly like what everyone from north of the Mason-Dixon Line thought the South looked like.

Near stagnant water, dense swamp vegetation, trees and undergrowth so tightly packed that little light entered, all topped off with a covering of Spanish moss that hung over everything like decayed tinsel.

And the smell.

And the bubbles of swamp gas that our minimal movement freed from the bottom.

And the flies.

Images of Southern movies from *Suddenly Last Summer* and *Hush, Hush Sweet Charlotte* to *In the Electric Mist* and *Southern Comfort* pushed into my mind and wouldn't move.

The thought of stepping off the boat to explore occurred to neither of us. While we saw no alligators – nor anything else – there were splashes, sudden swirls of water, bird and animal sounds and rustlings in the undergrowth that rendered us speechless.

I don't know what Dolly was thinking about, but I was thinking of the early settlers who came upon scenes like this and thought they could make a home here. That gave me a new level of admiration for them.

Still without a word, Dolly expertly backed the boat to the river entrance and told me to drop the anchor.

The water and air was clearer here, and we were free from the oppressive *Pigeons from Hell* atmosphere. Here was clean and bright and the sounds were normal, and a gentle breeze confirmed it as our picnic spot.

I brought the cooler up from the cabin and handed Dolly a Mountain Dew. We put the food on the table at the back deck and sat and watched the river in silence. We sat that way for nearly five minutes until I broke the silence.

"Nice boat handling," I said. "Backing out of that could not have been easy."

She raised her can like a toast and smiled.

We picked at the fruit before making a serious start on the food.

Northaw

After a few bites, Dolly seemed to relax.

"I don't know what's going on here, and it's equally intriguing, exasperating, and terrifying."

I waited for her to go on.

"That was one of the creepiest places I've been, and I've been up inlets all over this area."

I smiled and nodded agreement.

"That nightmare not withstanding, we've got a lot to talk about," she said, in her determined fashion. "Starting with that phantom steamboat in the picture."

I put my sandwich down.

"Okay," I began. "There are several possibilities. First, it's an anomaly – a trick of the light, a reflection of something in the mist. Secondly, it could be a tourist boat, or a leisure boat on its way to or from repair, refueling, or something like that. Are there still tourist steamboats on the Tombigbee?"

"No."

"Ah. Well, it could be digital artifacts or even a fault with the printer."

"Do you have your phone?" Dolly asked, and I handed it to her.

She turned it over to look at the lens and blew on it.

I laughed.

"It's not 'The Sphinx' – the Poe story about the insect mistaken for a monster," I said.

She activated the camera and enlarged the photo to look at the picture more closely.

"Something's there," she said.

"Okay. We now know that it's not the printer."

She gave me a filthy look.

"It does look a bit less like smokestacks than on the print, but that begs the question, what is it?"

"The other possibilities are," I continued, "that Lahoma – real or ghost – did some sort of projection, or – "

Dolly looked up.

"Or, we're the mad ones and there's nothing unusual on the photo."

I said this deadpan, and it took a second for her to realize I was teasing her. She was about to shout at me, but I interrupted.

"The truth is, this scares me, too. But it will have an explanation."

We continued our lunch. It was a bright, warm day with only the occasional pleasure boat heading up towards Gainesville and nothing on the Tuscaloosa branch.

"Those Choctaw legends – " Dolly began.

"The shilombish, shilup and the ishkitini? Well, if you want to go down the legends route, there are a few things that fit in that category," I said.

"Lahoma has talked a lot about Jody. Did you notice that she never refers to Jody as he or she? It's always Jody."

Dolly shook her head.

"I'm thinking that Lahoma and Jody are the same: one the shilup and one the shilombish, who remains on earth," I explained.

"So, we might be seeing the Jody side of Lahoma?"

I nodded, and Dolly held up her arm to show me her hair standing.

"Do you believe that?" she asked.

"Does it matter if I do if Lahoma/Jody does? Besides, you see Lahoma, too. And hear her.

"On the plus side, she's not frightening or threatening," I continued. "And, like you said, she wants to tell her story."

Dolly thought.

"But what is the story? A plantation, masters and slaves, cotton and tobacco, the river – what's the point?"

"Does there need to be one other than just *telling* it?" I asked.

She was silent, then erupted.

"This is ridiculous. We're treating her as some antebellum spirit, and we're all caught up in late New Age claptrap."

Dolly was right, and I was about to say so but then she said:

"Except. . ."

I waited.

"Except – ?"

"Except, I found a mention of a Francis Moran in a Mobile newspaper. It's in my notes at home. I'll show you when we get back. Basically, it was an announcement from an 1868 *Press-Register*. That said Francis "Buster" Moran had purchased a steamboat in a sale of boats commandeered by the Union Army during the occupation."

The first solid peg in Lahoma's story, but I was uncertain of the implications, as was Dolly having held on to that nugget until now.

"That *is* good news, isn't it?"

Northaw

19 I never get tired of comin' here. I mean, Northaw's home, but this is like watchin' the whole world. It don't rise and fall since they built the dams, but people and things still move on the river to all sorts of places. Everything comes and goes and it's the center of everything.

You make me laugh, Ben. 'Course it's the center. From where you and I are sittin', right now, everything stretches out. Marengo County, Sumter County, Green County, the state, the whole country, the whole world, and we're here in the middle.

No, I don't come here to watch the stars. I'm at Northaw and you can't see them from there. Only small patches. I never went into the fields at night – well, why do you think?

Always with the questions, Ben. Why don't you just listen? I've told you everything you want to know – 'cept of course, the last bit, an' you'll get that.

Yes, you know all about me. Things I never told anyone else, 'cept Jody, of course.

What you need to learn is that there are more ways of knowing things than just by asking questions. You get told things everyday that you can't see are important, but they are important to the person who tells you.

Your question should be why is this important *to him*?

When you're a slave, your mind isn't full of things about you. There is no point in havin' dreams, or wantin' things. You realize that even if you had them, they wouldn't do you any good.

We had all sorts of slaves at Northaw. Some were always angry, and some were truly broken, but in the middle there were people like Rufus, Jonah and Peony. They were good at what they did and were respected for it in a funny way. Mam tried to teach me that, but I didn't really learn it until that night Petey tried to kiss me.

After that, I saw that my nonsense wouldn't get me anywhere, and more, it wouldn't make me any happier. Peony and the others did their jobs and sort of floated above everything else: the arguments, worryin' about who had what or who got more.

We'd seen what happened to people who behaved like that. I've told you 'bout the 'portant ones but there were others who were forgotten pretty quickly because no one liked havin' them around. Their goin' was quiet. They were sold or traded and sometimes ran away.

Because of Monsieur, Mam and I felt pretty sure we wouldn't be sold, but we didn't know for sure. If something happened to Monsieur, Madame would want to get rid of us pretty quick. I just hoped she choose to sell me and not give me to the gators. Mam told me not to be silly, that wouldn't happen. Madame might not like us, but she liked what we did, and she trusted us.

Northaw

I didn't expect what happened.

No, it's okay, Ben. You see why I like to think of good things, an' there are quite a few of them if you look.

Like what?

Well, let me talk some more about that little boat ride you and Dolly took.

This was no pleasure trip, was it? You were looking for Northaw. You won't find it up Doom Creek – as I think you found out. There never was anything good up there. You could have got yourselves killed. If your boat hit a deadhead, or rock, you'd been stuck there with the gators and snakes. An' no one likes bein' there after dark when the meaner animals come out.

Good thing you came out when you did. An' while you were driftin' by the river in the sun enjoyin' the day, did your Creek tell you her plans for you?

Oh, she's got them all right, an' when she's ready you'll find yourself sittin' on a front porch mindin' the baby before you realise she's got you under her spell.

Might not be all bad, though.

The thing is, don't fight it. Them that does is never happy. Peony used to say that getting' along was like cookin' – you needed to know when to use salt and when to use sugar. Sometimes you had to use pepper, but don't do it too much!

Is it because of my descriptions of it that you want to find Northaw? Or, are you jus' tryin' to *prove* that it's a true story? That I ain't just some cuckoo makin' things up?

Well, if you want to find Northaw, you can't just head up every stream and slough. That's what you were doing there, wasn't it?

People did always have trouble findin' it, going up all the inlets and gettin' lost. Some of those sloughs go up for more than two miles since the dams was built. There ain't nothin' up there now. It's either fallen down or is underwater.

Is it that important that it's real? Maybe the question you should be askin' is *why* does it matter if it's real? Isn't the idea of it enough? A mystery?

No? All right.

If what I've told you is true, then you will want evidence – an' that's what you've been after since I came to you. Ben's dates. Ben's names. Ben's facts. All your questions is in that direction.

Suppose it's not true? Was there never anyone like Monsieur Lefever, Madame, Pierre François, Peony, Jonah and the others? Ask yourself if they *sound* real.

What? Dolly the Creek found Mr. Moran in Mobile? There you go. He was real. Now, she's goin' to ask if it were the same Buster Moran who was at Northaw. Of course, knowing about him doesn't prove anything about anyone else, so you're no better off.

Northaw

Yes, it means it's more likely, but tell me, in your experiences and travels, isn't it the unlikely things that are more likely? Aren't those the things that give you something to write about?

Ben, I'm just tellin' you things you already know, but it's a side you don't listen to. There's more than one voice in your head – and probably in Dolly's, too, though I wouldn't want to bet on it – try listening to them. They can be just as much help as your dates and facts.

It can be tricky because sometimes they're not just voices in your head.

Have you ever done something and the moment before it happened, you knew it was right? That it would work?

I've heard men talkin' about shootin' – sometimes a rifle, sometimes a bow and arrow – an' they'd say that before they pulled the trigger or let the arrow fly, they *knew* it would hit its target. They *knew*. No question. They knew.

You ever 'sperienced that? I thought so. How did it feel? Great, yes – and natural. *It was right*.

You want to find Northaw? I can tell you how to find it. Forget your head and travel like that arrow. It knows where it's goin' – an' so will you. Take the route that you see.

Trust me or don't. What have you got to lose?

I know you have to get back on the road again, so next time, I'll finish my story, an' we can both go our own way, that will leave you and Dolly free to decide what to do next.

Northaw

Ben's Notes

It wasn't easy to focus on what Lahoma had said about Northaw and its people. Her comments about objectivity, evidence and facts – though expressed in her quaint fashion – were a big distraction. What she said about finding Northaw resonated, too. I understood the sensation she described about knowing when something was going to work. Shooting an arrow or firing a rifle were good examples, but there were others.

People can struggle to undo a lock. They try rattling, jiggling, spraying with graphite or WD 40 and nothing works. Until. Until something in their heads changes and they put the key in, turn it, and the door opens. It's a common experience with technologies simple and complex, but somehow, it happens. Ghosts in the machines?

My own experience of that was with an old mechanical typewriter that I was trying to get working. I'd wrestled with one bit of the backspace mechanism for a week. Then, one morning, something in my mind was different, and I just fixed it. Easily.

Could this help me find Northaw as Lahoma suggested?

The topic I didn't want to address was Dolly.

Lahoma was right, I was attracted to her, and she seemed to enjoy my company and spent a few dozen gallons of gas for the boat on me.

She hadn't made any decisive move. Perhaps that was because she knew I'd be leaving soon. If I didn't go, what would I do in Demopolis?

ଽ

Looking at my notes, I've got pages of local color, some superficial history, cracker-barrel philosophy, and an anachronistic girl I still don't know what to make of.

Dolly thinks I don't care about facts, and Lahoma thinks I care too much about them.

But facts are the world of life – and who knows what world Lahoma is living in?

The way I see it, the world needs both the mystery-makers and those who solve them.

Which is more entertaining? More beneficial? Which do we learn most from; which gives us more satisfaction?

Did Mr. Carterer kill Mr. Skitters? Was Mr. Wilson killed in self-defense? Did the slaves run away and make a new life for themselves, or will they one day have their skeletons discovered when Daub's Swamp is drained to build the foundations of a new provincial capitol building in five hundred years' time?

Dolly and I are talking about it in 2023.

If we write about it – a piece of fiction (me) or a scholarly historical paper (Dolly) – which one will be read in a hundred years?

※

I met Dolly for dinner at a Chinese restaurant she said was new. The whole time I was trying to read the menu, she was asking questions.

Did I ask her about the smokestack in the picture? When I told her, no, I think she was ready to walk out, but she was hungry and talked about mentioning the restaurant in a blog.

"Why not?"

"I learn more when she just talks."

I told her about the different attitudes she'd talked about, and the incident of falling on the stairs.

"What use is that?" Dolly demanded.

"It's a good story. It gives insight into the people."

"But we don't know that they were people!" she nearly screamed which brought a waiter to the table to refill our teacups.

"I told her that you'd found Buster Moran."

"What did she say to that?"

I was afraid Dolly would ask that.

"She asked why that mattered, and how could we be sure it was the same Buster Moran?" I said.

I could see Dolly wrestling with her reply.

"We'll find some more names," she said, surprisingly calmly. "I think you were right about that: the first one will unleash a lot more. I've got a lead on a J. Wilson from Mobile who disappeared around 1856. It's a common name, but it's a lead."

Dozens of dishes and pots of food arrived in succession, and we relaxed. I told Dolly more of what Lahoma said about Doom Creek and the lengths of the sloughs.

"That's an apt name," she said. "It was a genuinely creepy place. You know, when I got home, I had a long shower. I felt it sticking to me, even after our nice picnic in the sun."

And then it happened.

Dolly reached across the table and took my hand. I tried not to react, and she didn't seem to notice anything, but I could sense my plans unraveling.

"Look, Lahoma might be a whack-job; this whole escapade nothing more than blue smoke and antebellum mirrors, but it's been fun," she said, not moving her hand.

"We'll see what she comes up with tomorrow," I said, turning my hand over under hers. "Want to come?"

I gave her hand a squeeze.

"Better not. She won't be as open with me around."

Simultaneously, we withdrew our hands and continued with our meal.

"What's your next project?"

"Not having gone to school in Demopolis, I got interested in education here and am starting to look into that," she said. "Did you know that there was a place here called the Marengo Female Institute?"

"No, but I have heard of the Marengo Military Academy."

Dolly thought a moment.

"That would make a good pair of stories. I could probably sell them to neighboring county papers, too. Maybe get a podcast interview."

I laughed.

"This would be a nice life if we didn't always have to hustle," I said. "Have you done a piece on the old hotels that used to be here? I think most of them were just for salesmen, brokers and dealers, and the odd plantation owner."

She smiled.

"The plantation owners would have gone to the Demopolis Hotel – now the Demopolis Inn Apartments," she said, in a mock snooty voice.

"The other one I've heard about was on Franklin opposite the passenger depot," I said.

"Where was that?"

"At the corner of Commissioners."

"Where I lost Lahoma."

"That's it," I said. "Maybe she has a room there."

She gave a dark smile which turned into a laugh as she realized that there was no longer anything on that intersection.

"That's what's fascinating about this town," she said. "There is less here now than ever. It's like old people who know more dead people than living ones. All those lost places have stories."

I put my chopsticks down and looked at Dolly. She's talented, determined, and dedicated to preserving the memories that make history, and making history accessible.

It strikes me that I will probably be saying goodbye to both Dolly and Lahoma in a few days.

Hitting the road again better be worth it.

"Maybe by this time tomorrow, we'll have some more answers, and maybe some facts for you."

Northaw

20

Now that Ben and the Creek understand things, I can tell Ben the rest of it. How I did get my chance to ride on a steamboat. It was an exciting trip, but a sad one too, as I had to say goodbye to Jonah and Buck, and Badger, and Peony. Sayin' goodbye to her near broke my heart.

When I said goodbye to Madame, she acted as though she'd never met me before, an' that didn't bother me at all. It was sad to leave Northaw and I didn't know what was comin', but Mam was comin' with me, and for what it was worth, Pierre François, too. He was known as Peter now which took some gettin' used to hearin', but, of course, I was now callin' him Master Lefever.

We were both twenty now, and he was ready to begin his growed up life. He was marryin' the daughter of a plantation owner near Coffeeville. As Mam explained it, we'd be working for Pierre François – something like a wedding gift to them from Monsieur.

Mam and I had very little to take with us, but there were all sorts of pots, pans, China, glass, cutlery and furniture that made its way from Northaw to the house near Coffeeville in the weeks before we went.

River Bend wasn't a particularly good name for a plantation. Madame called it "dull, like the people who lived in it." I didn't care how dull they were as long as they were good to Mam an' me. I even hoped that Pierre

François would be happy an' that Miss Belinda would be good to him.

While the family and the white managers were pleased, there were whisperings that Mr. Tucker was a lazy plantation owner who didn't much care how people were treated as long as the cotton made it to Mobile. That kind of talk made me scared, and I didn't tell Mam lest it upset her before she got there.

Everything and everyone seemed upset then. The plantation was still recovering from the drought of fifty-four. It went on and on. Crops died, no steamboats could move. The cotton warehouses were full, and people were sayin' that bales were piled up all along the river. Men said that there were steamboats sittin' on the bottom up an' down the Tombigbee just waiting for some water to come along an' float them.

I heard Peony say that no money was comin' in so the food had to be made to go further an' even if there was money, nothin' to buy had come up from Mobile, an' corn and wheat crops had dried up.

People had to stop buildin' because there was no nails, or hardware accordin' to Jonah who was then afraid of bein' sold just so Monsieur could get some cash.

It wasn't until October that the rains came an' while there was flooding, things were growin', and the river boats were movin' again.

This made for happier times when Pierre François' engagement to Miss Belinda Tucker was publicly announced. There was a lot of back and forth to Coffeeville which was a hundred miles away. I don't know how far that is, but if the steamboats didn't run at night – and not many did – it could take nearly a week for Madame or Monsieur to go down to River Bend and back. I didn't mind Madame being gone for a long time, but things were always better when Monsieur was around.

It was a good thing that the river was flowin' again as Madame needed things to wear at the weddin' an' Monsieur even bought some new boots and a blue waistcoat. I always thought he looked handsome.

Pierre François talked to me once or twice about all that was goin' on.

"There are going to be big changes, here and all over the South," he said, sounding grown up and important. "Best to get ahead of them."

I didn't know what that meant, but it sounded serious. One day, when he walked past me in the house he said, "I'm glad you and your Mam are coming to Coffeeville. It will be good to have familiar faces down there."

I didn't know what to say, so I just said, "I wish you happiness, Master Pierre."

He gave somethin' of a smile but didn't look as confident as when he talked about "big changes."

"When I'm married, you'll have to call me Mr. Lefever, and my wife Mrs. Lefever, or Madame."

I bobbed like Madame taught me, and said, "Of course, Master Pierre."

He almost smiled when he said, "Thank you, Lahoma."

The families had agreed on an autumn wedding, then it became one around Christmas, and it was finally set for March tenth. I don't know why there was a delay, just a lot of huffin' and tuttin', but eventually we were told it was time to go. I'd had my things in a peach basket since I was first told I'd be leaving Northaw.

Early in the morning, it was a Sunday, Madame, Monsieur, Master Pierre, Mam and me got on a flatboat with trunks, baskets, boxes an' bags, along with our blankets and cloaks. Several slaves were comin' with us to help carry things an' I think they would be staying at River Bend, too. There were also the boat slaves who'd be takin' the flatboat back to Northaw.

I started cryin' as I walked down to the flatboat. Even though I'd be with Mam, and travelin' with people I knew, Northaw had been all I knew. I'd watched it built, growin' up an' establishin' itself in the world, like an old friend.

I knew as I watched it disappear behind the branches and the Spanish moss as we slid down the inlet that I'd never see it again. Mam saw my tears and wrapped me in my blanket so no one else could see. She remind me that I was now twenty years old and would have my own

Northaw

responsibilities at River Bend, unlike at Northaw where I did a bit of this and a bit of that, and life was easier than in a lot of places people talked about.

When we got off the flatboat, Mam, seeing my tears were still there, held me close.

"It's all life, child, you take what comes," she said, then added, "and it's comin' now."

I looked up and could see smoke rising above the fields and trees. This was exciting, even feelin' as I did. I was goin' for at trip on a steamboat!

We sat near the cotton that was stacked up and waited. Men stood around smokin' cigars and talkin' about how high the river was, and that it would be a quick trip down to Mobile.

I asked Mam how long it would take to Coffeeville.

"It's a long way," she said. "It will take all night and then some."

I was cold, but sittin' between the bales, we were out of the wind – and then the steamer appeared with its side wheels splashin'.

The men got the slaves ready to start movin' the cotton, and the white passengers came out of their carriages as we watched it pull up to the shore – which was now over the banks due to the flood. Men put planks across and the passengers got on and went up to the saloon, where there would be food and bedrooms.

We saw the Lefevers go onboard, Pierre François lookin' handsome. Once the passengers were aboard, the cotton was loaded, and then the slaves.

We couldn't go upstairs, but found places between the bales and the sides of the engine place where we could get a little heat an' sat on the wooden deck. I wanted to watch us float away from Demopolis, but the bales covered the guards.

We heard the engine, smelled the cotton and the fire in the boiler, and listened to the splashes and sounds of the wheel creakin' an' strainin'.

There was nothin' to do and I couldn't go see anythin'.

"There aren't many times you can do nothin'," Mam said. "Give thanks for it now. You'll be busy enough, soon. In an hour or two, we can have some of the food we brought."

Later, I could hear music upstairs with the noise of clapping and the sound of shoes on the floor.

Some slaves were sleepin' on top of the cotton where it wasn't piled too high. I heard someone say there were more than a thousand bales on board. I'd only seen that much when I went with Monsieur and some slaves to a warehouse.

Don't ask me why I went, Ben. Probably jus' to carry somethin'.

It's a funny thing, having nothing to do. I got to day dreamin' an thinking about watchin' Northaw bein' built, an' tried to remember how Peony taught me things in the kitchen and wondered if I'd have to cook meals for the Tuckers. It weren't long before Mam gave me some food and we ate, and laughed about some of the things we'd seen an' heard, but it was dark now and getting very cold. We were lucky to feel some of the heat from the engines.

"We're runnin' all night," Mam said. "They do that when the river's so high they can't see the normal landin's."

Just then, there was a crackin' an' snappin' as we hit tree branches. Goin' round a bend, Mam said.

It were cold, and then it were wet as the wind came up and cold rain, then sleet hit us. We held up our blankets to protect us like a tent, but then the water starts sloshin' around the deck and we have to stand up. The boat turns around bends and is pushed by the wind, the whistle is blastin' and the wind shifting because we're turnin'.

We hug each other and press ourselves against the wall of the boiler room and cling to each other. We nearly fall asleep standing up we're there so long.

Upstairs, there's noise and laughin' as the boat shakes like a cart goin' too fast on a rough road.

We move a little and there's a small shelf between some cotton bales. I wanted to go there earlier, but Mam said the bales could move suddenly and crush us because they're so heavy. We wasn't gettin' much heat from the boilers as it were all blowin' away, so we huddled on the cotton with our wet blankets an' shared an apple from the fruit cellar.

I must have fallen asleep, but when I woke, there was lots of noise and Mam wasn't next to me.

I was just about to scream, "Mam!" when someone else yelled "Fire!" an' there were rushin' all over the place. When I looked, I could see there were smoke everywhere and flames at the back of the boat.

There was crashin' into trees, and bales fallin' into the river, and more shoutin' and screamin'. We must have run into the bank because there was a big lurch as everyone fell forwards, and more bales fell. I could hear glass and china breakin' upstairs, and people callin' to each other.

I climbed down and started to look for Mam, but was pushed out of the way and near bundled along the deck until someone grabbed me.

"Lahoma!"

It were Pierre François. He pulled me with him and we climbed over bales and stuff. It were all in the dark 'cept for the light of the flames. The boat swung again and hit more trees, and we fell over on top of each other.

"Come on!" he shouted, and pulled me with a strength I didn't think he had.

Somehow, we got to the side of the boat that was along the bank. People were jumping into the water and crying, when suddenly, Pierre François pulled off his coat, wrapped it around me and seemed to throw me onto a tree branch.

"Thank you, Petey," I managed to whisper, and he nodded an' gave his grin as the steamship moved away from the bank.

I sat there dumbfounded, clingin' to the branch. Then I realized Jody was next to me, an' I knew things would be all right. I clung to that branch for dear life, and watched the boat, half in flame, as it slid away from us.

"Stay there!" I heard Pierre François shout, as that whole world drifted away.

Northaw

Ben's Notes

"I hope you asked her some questions?" Dolly demanded, when I told her the story in the diner the next morning. "Why didn't you call me last night?"

"I didn't need to," I said, calmly. "It all makes sense of a sort."

And it did. I was in no state to talk to anyone when she finished. I needed to get home and write it down while I could still remember. Anyway, when I'd turned to Lahoma to question her, she had gone.

Dolly looked at me with a combination of disbelief and fury, then turned to the pages I'd written and read them as she ate a sausage.

"Names!" she said, exasperated.

"We've got a date. That tells us most of what we need."

Dolly turned back to the beginning, and her eyes opened wide as she understood.

"This is the – "

"Yes," I said, as excited as she was. "The most famous wreck on the Tombigbee. *And*, I think I can find Northaw."

૱

Less than two hours later, we were aboard the *Dolly* and making our way upriver.

"Did she finally tell you where it was?" Dolly asked, having calmed down.

We'd picked up food, stopped at the marina to get gas, and continued upriver turning at the Tuscaloosa branch.

"There should be an old inlet between here and the Glover's Ferry landing," I said.

"You haven't even got a map, Choctaw," she said, but with good humor.

We slowed, scanning the shore.

"How are we going to find anything?" she asked. "It's been a hundred seventy years and the water's fifty feet higher. It's not called Daub's Swamp for nothing."

We looked at every inlet and drew quite near to the shore.

"You can be further out, Dolly," I said. "There's no telling what's under here or how deep it is."

"There!" she called, and cut the engine.

She aimed the boat towards the mouth of a fairly wide inlet, and I looked to the opposite banks and the area either side.

Northaw

It looked the same as the others we'd passed with thick underbrush, large trees and thick Spanish moss. It looked beautiful, but it didn't look right – but how would I know? It might only exist in my imagination.

We were stopped now ,and the water of the inlet was still – like everything around it.

It was wildly beautiful, like the lake we had visited. I expect we were both watching for alligators, but nothing moved.

I stood next to Dolly by the wheel and put my arm around her, and she gently leaned into me.

"Shall we try it?" she asked.

I shook my head.

"No, this isn't it."

She sighed but started the engine.

"Some Choctaw memory rattling the DNA??"

I laughed.

"Some Choctaw memory *not* rattling the DNA."

Dolly smiled, shook her head and reversed back into the river.

"This is new territory for me," she said.

"I thought you'd explored all of this?"

"Not literally," she laughed. "Sometimes, I'm not literal, you know. No, this is myth, legend, weirdness stuff."

"You ought to get out more," I teased. "Look and listen and the truth will emerge."

She still shook her head.

"I've said this before: I value evidence as much as you do, but our Indian ancestors knew that the earth speaks, too," I said. "Don't worry, I'm not going hoodoo, I won't be shaking bones, or making bottle trees, but we have our imaginations for a reason. Myth and legend, the imagination and the real world come together sometimes."

We moved along at a walking pace.

"Stop!" I said, more loudly than I meant. "Sorry. There."

There was a hooked inlet, similar to the one we had turned into on our first boat trip, nearly invisible to passing traffic.

Dolly backed the boat and nosed towards the opening before cutting the engine. We glided into the entrance before stopping.

"This is it," I said, more calmly than even I expected.

Northaw

I felt no excitement or triumphalism, but a certainty that this was what we were looking for. The arrow had shot home.

Dolly climbed off the seat and stood by me and took my hand. We looked up the twisting course but could only see a few hundred feet before it bent into a new direction.

"I think you're right, Ben," she said. "Look, we're drifting out already. With these flooded areas, there is relatively little movement out of them, but this one has a current, small, but it's moving us."

"Spring-fed," we said, at the same time.

"Just as Lahoma had said."

"I'll agree with spring-fed for now."

She started the engine, and we inched carefully up the stream, stopping at the bend.

"Do you want to risk it, or shall we get out and walk?" she asked.

"Pull up and I'll tie it off," I said. "And don't forget your revolver."

೮೧

Dolly had brought the photocopies of the maps and sketches I had made based on Lahoma's story.

"Let's give this an hour," Dolly said. "I want to be back before dusk. If we find anything, I'll buy you dinner."

We had stout boots on. Dolly's had far more wear than mine. I set off on a course heading into the woods at about twenty degrees away from the inlet; once again, the machete proved useful.

"Shouldn't we follow the stream?" Dolly asked.

"The stream runs by the orchard. The house is east of it," I said.

"Let me guess: Lahoma told you – the maps sure as hell didn't."

"No, they just show swamp – which it has been since it was first permanently flooded in the early 1900s, then it got much deeper it the 1950s."

I stopped.

"Give me the notebook," I said, holding out my hand.

There were now more than a hundred pages of notes, maps and downloaded photos, mostly of Demopolis and steamboats. I went through them.

"Look, this is a recent satellite picture, I found online this week."

"I've seen this. This place is seventy percent water."

"Turn back a page."

She did.

"That one was taken in 1987 but in low water conditions," I said, standing next to her and pointing. "There's the lake there, and you can see the stream better."

"It's certainly a lot drier," she admitted.

"Now, what would that have looked like with no locks and the water fifty feet lower?"

She nodded.

"It could easily be farmland," she said. "Where do you think the house was?"

I gave a short laugh.

"I have no idea. There's not a hint of anything, but over here – where we're headed, the green of the trees is darker."

"Meaning?"

"I don't know," I said, remembering Lahoma's words. "It just looks a likely place. It *feels* right, and those hardwood trees may have been planted and self-seeded.

"I looked up the soil here and were it not flooded, it would be excellent for agriculture. Clay and sandy loams, rich in nutrients, holds moisture and – ironically – good drainage."

"*Geographers!*" she exclaimed, like an expletive. "Pity about the flooding."

We moved on, with me a few steps ahead of her, slicing undergrowth as I went.

"Ah ha!" I said, stopping suddenly.

Dolly, still moving forward, bumped into me. I bent down and pulled a long square-head nail out of the ground and passed it to her.

She looked at it with surprise, then said:

"Yeah, right, this is just going to be lying on the ground after all this time."

"It's rusted enough," I said.

She flaked some rust off with her thumb.

"Not buying it."

I turned to face her.

"A wooden wall falls over. A plank breaks loose from the stud. The plank rots – possibly broken by something else falling on it – and the bit with a nail floats off, snags here, more wood rots off and a piece with the nail looses buoyancy, until now, there is just the nail left for us to find. That's why it's here and on the surface."

Dolly is silent for a moment before moaning:

"*I'm the historian here!*"

We laugh and move on, but after another twenty feet, Dolly grabs my arm and points.

"Dogwood – and magnolia."

The growth is dense here and we have to dodge Spanish moss as well as branches and whatever's underfoot. The damp rotting smells that we have been used to are more concentrated, but the ground underfoot is still firm and dry.

Dolly is making her way around a large clump of jewel weed about five feet high and nearly meeting the Spanish moss above when I hear her gasp. I follow her quickly and find her staring at a large area of vines and low growth covering a large undulating area of green punctuated with square brick pillars and chimneys.

We both stand still, silently gawping at the sight. My surprise was mitigated by my total belief that we'd find something, but Dolly appeared to be in astonished shock.

I opened the notebook to look at the sketches I'd made from Lahoma's descriptions and tried to orient where we were in relation to the house. It took a bit of fiddling, but it became clear.

I nudged Dolly and showed her what I thought we were looking at.

"Then we should see what should be the front of the house from over there," she said, and we hacked through the brush.

What remained of the curved double brick staircase could be seen rising above the vegetation with patches of scored render still clinging to it. There were chimneys, pillars leaning off true in the soft ground, stumps of pillars, and growth-covered mounds of – what? Rubble? Ash?

I was watching a small movement in the vegetation on the old staircase – swamp rabbit, possum, fox? – when three things happened in rapid succession.

The first was the sound of a steam whistle, the sort I'd only heard on excursion river boats. The second, a rapid rustling behind us. We only saw the cause because our heads were turned towards the river. Finally, there were two rapid, explosive, reports from Dolly's revolver followed by thrashing and the sight of a dead alligator.

I squeezed her arm as I realized what a close call it had been.

"You saved my – "

Something caught my eye.

"Look! There's something on the stairs – "

Northaw

She raised the pistol, taking aim towards the movement. Then, she very slowly lowered the pistol, and we watched as Lahoma stood on the steps and raised her hand to us and walked proudly to where the balcony entrance had been.

We looked, as if in a dream, until another piercing blast of the steamboat whistle shook us from our trance. We looked uncomprehendingly at each other, then back towards the stairs, but Lahoma was gone.

Northaw

Dolly's Epilogue

We hardly knew what to do. We were spooked. Totally spooked, we clung to each other.

As fans of ghost stories, we both knew the story of the two English ladies who thought they saw Marie Antoinette at Versailles in the early 1900s, so Ben and I agreed to say nothing about what we'd seen and heard until we'd both written our accounts and could compare them.

On the way back, we were elated with the discovery and shaken by both the near-miss with the alligator and by what we thought we saw on the steps.

It was an odd silence in the boat on the way home. The twenty-first century sound of the engine contrasted with the timeless sound of the water. We felt simultaneously close and distant. I drove the boat, dropping Ben at the landing before heading down to The Cove. He went straight back to his room to write up what he'd seen. I had to wait, delayed and distracted by dinner with my parents and chats about the neighbors and local politics, so I couldn't settle down to write until later.

We met for lunch the next day and exchanged our accounts, and there was little difference between them. We even agreed on what Lahoma was wearing. Used to writing, our versions were full, and while we'd noticed a few different things, the details of our observations and impressions were the same.

Inevitably, we asked, "What's next?" and Ben's reply shocked and saddened me.

"It's time to get back on the road," he said, and I nearly screamed at him.

"How can you leave this mystery – this discovery?!" I demanded.

He paused, and, maddeningly, ate his pecan pie. I was about to strangle him right there in the diner.

"Dolly, can't you see it's all down hill from here?" he asked, oblivious to my anger.

I was taken off guard.

"What do you mean?"

"What's next?" he asked. "We either prove what we already know or disprove what we've seen. Northaw gets stripped bare in all its ruin, and people get charged to see what it was never meant to be."

He stood up and went to the register.

"*Really?!*" I exclaimed, hurrying to follow him out the door and into the light and towards the river.

Northaw

He stopped and looked at me with infuriating patience.

"You research it if you want to," he said. "You're looking for history; I'm looking for a story – a tale, or yarn of the old South. Not as noble as your intention, I know, but more entertaining, and probably more memorable, and I've got it."

I couldn't speak.

"What Lahoma said is probably as true as anything you'll find," he continued. "Peony probably was 'Monsieur's' half sister. And, he and Pierre François were probably killed at Shiloh, but what would be gained from proving or disproving it?

"You may have better luck finding River Bend and working backwards from that, Dolly," he said. "For me, I like a good mystery. It's good to have one to think about from time to time, and this one I can return to for the rest of my life."

"But it's all been pointless," I said, more impatiently than I probably should. "We've got *nothing!* I wanted something I could build a reputation on that more than a hundred people might read. I've wasted weeks!"

As soon as I finished, I felt sorry for Ben. He didn't deserve a selfish tantrum. I was about to apologize but when I looked at him, he just stared at me with the biggest self-satisfied grin on his face that I'd ever seen – and he was *good* at them.

"Why are you looking so... *insufferably smug*?" I demanded.

And he laughed out loud - for too long – and I could feel my face get even redder.

"I admire your ambition, but it's not making you happy, Dolly," he said, in his gentlest voice. "You don't have your blessed facts, and I don't know if I have enough for a story, but it's been the biggest adventure I've had.

"Better than camping in Death Vally, or climbing Pike's Peak, better than nearly drowning in a Minnesota Cranberry bog, or even standing on the floor of the United States Senate," he said, pompously, and drew himself up and hooked his thumbs into an imaginary waistcoat.

Then his voice softened again.

"I learned more about where I grew up in the past few weeks than in twenty years of living here. We saw some interesting places, found a few lost ruins and had a good time on the river. We learned more about our heritage, and we might have talked to a ghost," he said.

I was softening but still skeptical, but then he stopped walking, took my hand and looked at me.

"Best of all, I met you."

I can't say that the world suddenly changed, and all rational thoughts vanished from my mind, but I did get a glimpse of what Ben was talking about.

The ruins we saw were real. The town was real. Ben was real. It was the truth that was illusive.

We walked along in silence the half mile down to the landing where we'd seen Lahoma and stood watching the river.

We'd held hands all the way. That simple act of seeking, now finding, connection had to me always been a sign of surrender – until now.

I wasn't ready for this. I had to get away from there before my emotions took over completely, but Ben, well he couldn't have been cooler. Calm. Confident. Solid.

I'd like to believe that he knew what I was thinking.

I dropped his hand.

"Good luck, Choctaw."

He gave me the lightest of kisses.

"I'll be back one day, Creek."

I'll be here, I thought.

By the same author

The Unvarnished Truth Series

On the Edge of Dreams and Nightmares
Circle of Vanity
Bickering
The Cardinal's Legacy

The Trumbull Chronicles

Fourscore and Upward
The Time of No Horizon
In an Age without Honor

Stories

Undivulged Crimes
Thoughts and Whispers
Clubs, Bills and Partisans

Other Novels

Nantucket Summer
Wachusett
The Camels of the Qur'an
The Countess Comes Home
Entrusted in Confidence
Lost Lady
Ardmore Endings
The Rock Pool

Parkman House is the imprint of Lattimer & Co. for contemporary American fiction.

Established in Philadelphia in 1870 by "Colonel" Jonah Lattimer, the Lattimer & Co. also includes the imprints of Defarge Frères and Editions Chaillot, both of Paris.